*A
Harlequin
Romance*

OTHER
Harlequin Romances
by BETTY NEELS

1361—SISTER PETERS IN AMSTERDAM
1385—NURSE IN HOLLAND
1409—SURGEON FROM HOLLAND
1441—NURSE HARRIET GOES TO HOLLAND
1465—DAMSEL IN GREEN
1498—FATE IS REMARKABLE
1529—TULIPS FOR AUGUSTA
1569—TANGLED AUTUMN
1593—WISH WITH THE CANDLES
1625—VICTORY FOR VICTORIA
1641—THE FIFTH DAY OF CHRISTMAS
1666—SATURDAY'S CHILD
1689—CASSANDRA BY CHANCE
1705—THREE FOR A WEDDING
1737—WINTER OF CHANGE
1761—STARS THROUGH THE MIST
1777—ENCHANTING SAMANTHA
1801—UNCERTAIN SUMMER
1817—THE GEMEL RING
1841—THE MAGIC OF LIVING

THE
MAGIC OF LIVING

by

BETTY NEELS

HARLEQUIN BOOKS   TORONTO
WINNIPEG

Original hard cover editon published in 1974
by Mills & Boon Limited.

© Betty Neels 1974

SBN 373-01841-X

Harlequin edition published January 1975

Printed in Canada

1841

CHAPTER ONE

THE nursery of Little Dean House was no longer used as such, but its rather shabby comfort, coupled with the knowledge that Nanny Bliss would be sitting by its cheerful little fire in the old-fashioned grate, the very epitome of security, and when necessary, sympathy, made it a retreat to which every member of the Birch family went at one time or another.

The elder daughter of the family flung open its door now; she had hunted all over the garden for Arabella without success, only to remember after ten minutes' futile poking and peering in the rather untidy, overgrown garden which surrounded the rambling house that she had heard her cousin say that she would help the twins finish their jigsaw puzzle during the afternoon, and that, she knew from experience, would be in the old nursery.

All three of them were on the floor, she perceived, as she shut the door behind her and crossed the room to where Edmund and Erica, with Arabella between them, were sprawling on their knees. The twins were ten years old; already showing signs of the family good looks, but their cousin bore no resemblance to her relations, for she had no looks worth mentioning; indeed, beside the golden prettiness of her older cousin, her unremarkable features and pale brown hair stood no chance at all; something which didn't bother her overmuch; she had lived with her aunt and uncle since she had been orphaned at the age of five, and over the years had become accustomed to living in Hilary's shade. They got on tolerably well together, and if the elder girl had the lion's share of praise for her pretty face, her undoubtedly clever mind, and her charm of manner, Arabella hadn't minded that either; at least not much. Hilary was the daughter of the house and as such expected – and got – everything she wanted. Arabella could quite see that she could hardly expect to receive the same attention for herself and she was grateful for the rather vague affection accorded her by her aunt and uncle – after all, they had given her a pleasant home, a good education and had treated her as one of the family – well, almost, and now that she was twenty-two and a trained children's nurse and half way through her general training, it was only natural that her aunt should consider her capable of keeping an eye on the twins when they were home from school and she was herself on holiday or days off. It sometimes meant that she was the one to stay home if an expedition which didn't include the twins was planned, for Nanny Bliss, although barely in her sixties, was still not quite recovered from the 'flu, with all its attendant after-effects, and as Aunt Maud pointed out sensibly enough, the twins needed someone firm as well as patient; able to join in their activities and curb them in their more hair-raising adventures.

It was a pleasant autumn afternoon, and Arabella had hoped to go over to the doctor's house for tea and a game of tennis, but her aunt's hints at lunch had been strong enough for her to scotch this idea. She had resigned herself to entertaining the twins, who, for some reason known only to their mother, had been told to remain indoors. Arabella knelt between them now, her chin on her hands, studying the puzzle and tolerably content. She had learned years ago not to be sorry for herself and she had common sense enough to realize that not everyone could expect everything they dreamed of from life. She liked her work, she had a number of friends and a strong affection for her uncle and aunt as well as a sense of loyalty. She looked up now as her cousin came to a halt in front of her, and the better to talk, dropped to her knees too.

She said in a wheedling voice: "Bella, I want to talk to you."

Arabella fitted a particularly difficult piece into the puzzle. When Hilary called her Bella it meant that she wanted her to do something for her: partner some disappointed young man to the cinema or local dance because Hilary had something better to do – lend her something, or drive her somewhere, for Hilary couldn't drive; she hated it and declared that she had men friends enough to drive her wherever she wished to go, only just sometimes they weren't available, and then Arabella, who despite her unpretentious appearance, drove very well indeed, would be coaxed into getting out the car and taking her cousin to wherever it was she wanted to go. It could be a nuisance, but Arabella enjoyed driving and it had never entered her head to condemn her cousin for being selfish.

It wasn't any of these things now, though. Hilary went on: "Let's go over to the window," and ignoring the cries of protest from the two children, strolled to the other end of the room, calling a casual "Hi, Nanny," as she went. Arabella shook herself free from her cousins and joined her, waiting quietly to hear what Hilary had to say and thinking as she waited what a very pretty girl she was and how clever too. She was one of the Ward Sisters on the private wing at the same hospital at which Arabella was doing her training, and was popular with patients and doctors alike, being showered with gifts from the former and receiving a never-ending series of invitations from the latter, and on top of that, she was very good at her job. She turned her bright blue eyes upon her cousin now.

"Bella, remember when old Lady Marchant asked me if I'd go with that bus load of kids to that holiday camp in Holland – something to do with that society – she's the president or secretary, I can't remember – and I said I would, because after all, she's frightfully influential and all that – well, Dicky White" – Dicky was one of the adoring housemen who followed her around – "told me yesterday that the old girl had gone to Canada, so she won't know if I go on that dreary trip or not."

She smiled brilliantly and with great charm. "Go instead of me, darling – you know how good you are with brats. Besides that, Sister Brewster's going too, and you know I simply can't stand her – I should go mad."

Arabella didn't like Sister Brewster either. "They're

8

spastics," she reminded her cousin.

Hilary gave her a faintly impatient look. "Well, of course they are, ducky, that's why you'll be so marvellous with them – after all, you're children's trained." She nodded encouragingly, "You'll be just right."

"It's for two weeks," Arabella pointed out, and added reasonably, "and I don't really want to go, Hilary, my holidays are due and I'm going to stay with Doreen Watts – you know, in Scotland."

"Oh, lord, Bella, you can change your holidays and go a couple of weeks later – what's a couple of weeks?" Hilary waved an airy hand; she had long ago mastered the art of reducing everything which didn't directly concern herself to an unimportant level which she didn't need to worry about.

"Why don't you want to go?" asked Arabella. "Oh, I know about old Brewster, but what's the real reason?"

Hilary smiled slowly. "It's a secret, so don't breathe a word. You know that new honorary? the one with the dark hair and the hornrims?"

"Mr. Thisby-Barnes?" Arabella's voice was squeaky with surprise. "But he's married!"

Her cousin gave her a look of contemptuous affection. "Bella, you are a simpleton – a nice one, mind you – I do believe you still live in an age of orange blossom and proposals of marriage and falling in love."

"Yes," said Arabella simply.

"Well, darling, a lot of girls still do, I suppose, but one can have some fun while waiting for the orange blossom – and I'm not doing any harm. He and his wife don't get on, and I'm only going out to dinner with him."

"But can't you go out with him before you go with the children?"

Hilary frowned. "Look, darling, there's a dance he's taking me to – oh, don't worry, it's miles away from Wickham's, no one will ever know, and it comes slap in the middle of this wretched trip." She turned her beautiful eyes upon Arabella. "Bella, do help me out – I can wangle it so easily, and no one will mind. There are a thousand good reasons why I can't go at the last minute and they'll be only too glad if I can find someone to take my place – you." Which was true enough.

Arabella frowned, and the stammer which only became noticeable when she was deeply moved, became apparent. "You s-see, Hilary, I d-don't think you sh-should."

Her cousin smiled beguilingly. "Oh, Bella darling, I tell you it's all right. Anyway, I've promised to go and I can't break a promise."

"B-but you m-must have k-known that you were going with the children before you s-said you would go," stated Arabella baldly.

She studied her cousin's face, reflecting that Hilary had been like a big sister to her ever since she could remember – a rather thoughtless sister sometimes, but never unkind. That she was also completely selfish was a fact which Arabella had grown up with and accepted cheerfully; if she herself had been the pretty, pampered daughter of a well-to-do man she would undoubtedly have been selfish too. She watched a dimple appear in Hilary's cheek.

"Yes, I did," admitted her cousin, "but I knew you'd help me out." She added urgently, "You will, won't you, Bella?"

"All right," said Bella, "but I won't do it again, really I won't."

Her cousin flung an arm around her shoulders. "You're a darling – tell you what, I'll see if I can get Watts' holidays changed, then you can go home with her when you get back – how's that for a good idea?"

Arabella agreed that it was, provided that Doreen didn't mind, and suppose it wasn't convenient for her family? Hilary waved the idea away carelessly; she would arrange everything, she said airily. "And what's more," she promised, "I'll come back to Wickham's to-morrow with you, instead of waiting until the next day, then you can have the Triumph to drive us up and drive yourself back on your next days off."

A bribe – Arabella recognised it as such; she loved driving. One day, when she was a qualified nurse and earning more money, she intended to save up and buy herself a car, but until then she had to depend upon her uncle's kindness in lending her the Triumph which shared the garage with his Daimler. She said now: "That will be nice, thank you, Hilary," but Hilary, having got what she had come for, was already on her way to the door.

It was when the twins had been sent away to wash their hands for tea that Nanny, knitting endlessly, had

11

looked up from her work to say:

"You always were a bonny child, Miss Arabella, and far too kind-hearted. Miss Hilary always had what she wanted out of you, and still does; no good will come of it."

Arabella was putting the last few pieces of the puzzle in their places, but she paused to look at the cosy little figure in the old-fashioned basket chair. "Nanny dear, I don't mind a bit – did you hear what we were talking about?"

"Well enough. And what happens, young lady, if Miss Hilary should set eyes on a young man you fancied for yourself, eh? Do you let her have him?"

"Well," said Arabella matter-of-factly, "I can't imagine that happening, and if it did, what chance would I have, Nanny? No one ever looks at me when Hilary's there, you know – besides, I don't care for any of the men who fancy her."

"That's a vulgar expression," said Nanny repressively, "but one day, mark my words, Mr. Right will come along and you won't want to share him."

Arabella wasn't attending very closely; she asked eagerly:

"Nanny, do you believe in orange blossom and falling in love? You don't think it's old-fashioned?"

"How can anything be old-fashioned when it's been going on since the world began, Miss Arabella? You keep right on thinking that, and leave those queer young people in their strange clothes and hair that needs a good brush . . ." she snorted indignantly. "Let them think

12

what they like, they'll find out what they're missing, soon enough," she added darkly.

Arabella got up off her knees and went to look out of the window.

"I wonder if I shall like Holland," she hazarded. "The camp's somewhere in the middle." She sighed to herself; probably she would be alternately run off her feet and bored stiff, for Sister Brewster was twice her age and she had worked on her ward and hated every minute of it. It was a pity that Lady Marchant had ever had the idea of asking Wickham's Hospital to lend two of its nurses to accompany the children – just because she had been a patient there and had taken a fancy to Hilary – perhaps she thought she was conferring a favour, or more likely, she had had difficulty in recruiting anyone else.

"I think I'll go for a walk," said Arabella; she didn't want any tea, she felt all of a sudden out of tune with the world, a good walk would settle everything back into its right place again. After all, what did it matter if she went on holiday a couple of weeks later – and she liked children. Besides, it would be an opportunity to see another country, however limited the sightseeing would be.

She went down the back stairs and out of the kitchen door and through the little wicket gate at the bottom of the vegetable garden and so into the woods beyond. It was quiet there, the house stood equidistant between Great Sampford and Little Sampford, a mile or so away from the country road which connected these two villages, so that there was nothing but the quiet Essex

13

countryside around her. She wandered on, and presently came out on to the crossroads, where four lanes met and parted again to go to Finchingfield, Steeple Bumpstead, Cornish Hall End and, behind her, back to the Sampfords. She chose the way to Cornish Hall End, because it went through the neck of the woods once more and at its end she could take the path back through the trees.

It was September and warm for the time of year. Arabella pulled off the cardigan she had snatched up as she had left the house and walked on, wishing she was wearing something thinner than the cotton shirt and rather shabby tweed skirt she had on. There had seemed no point in wearing anything else when she had got up that morning; she had known in advance that she would be asked to pick fruit some time during the day, and later, when she would have changed, she had had the twins wished on her. Thinking about them reminded her of Hilary's request, and her pleasant little face became thoughtful – it was a pity that her cousin had got entangled with Mr. Thisby-Barnes, but Arabella knew from experience that it wouldn't help in the least if she were to argue with Hilary about him. Hilary had always done exactly what she wanted to do, in the most charming way possible, and would brook no interference.

Arabella dismissed the vexing matter from her mind, sensibly realizing that there was nothing to be done about it except hope that Hilary would tire of Mr. Thisby-Barnes as quickly as she had tired of so many other of her admirers. Having disposed of one worry, however, Arabella found her mind turning to another –

14

the bus trip with the children. She would have to find out more about it, and about a passport and what she was supposed to take in the way of clothes. It would be necessary to go and see Sister Brewster, who would probably hate her going just as much as she herself was beginning to.

She turned off the road and started back home, thinking vaguely now of all the things she would like to do and wondering if she would ever get the chance of doing half of them. She would like to marry, of course – some paragon whose hazy picture in her head was a splendid mixture of good looks and charm and endless adoration of her homely self, besides being possessed of sufficient money to give her all she should ever ask for. That she wasn't the kind of girl to ask for anything seemed beside the point, as did the fact that the young men of her acquaintance tended to treat her like a younger sister and seldom showed any sign of even the mildest interest in her. It would help, she thought a trifle wistfully, if Hilary were to marry and go and live somewhere sufficiently far away to leave her a clear field; not that that would help much, although there had been Jim Besley, a casualty officer at Wickham's who had shown signs of fancying her – he had driven her home for her days off, though, but Hilary had been home too, and although she had made no effort to charm him, he had had no eyes for Arabella after that. And there had been Tony Clark, a dull young man from the Path Lab – he had got as far as suggesting that he should take Arabella to the cinema one evening, only Hilary had come along just as he was getting down to details as to where they should meet, and somehow they didn't go after all. He took Hilary out instead and spent so much money on her entertainment that Arabella's kind heart was wrung by the sight of the economical meals of eggs and chips he was forced to live on in the canteen until pay day came round again.

She had walked rather further than she had intended; she got back to the house only just in time to get ready for dinner, and her aunt, meeting her in the hall as she went in, her mousy hair hanging untidily down to her waist, her cardigan slung anyhow round her shoulders, asked her with some asperity where she had been, and would have doubtless delivered a short, not unkind lecture on her appearance, if Hilary hadn't come running downstairs, looking like a fairytale princess, to rescue her with a few careless, charming words. Arabella gave her a grateful glance. Hilary was a dear, it was mean to feel annoyed, however faintly at having been coerced into taking her cousin's place on the children's outing; it was, after all, a small return for the kindness she had received from her cousin since she had gone, as a small, unhappy girl, to live with Hilary's parents.

She was still of the same mind the following morning as she drove the Triumph back to London with Hilary beside her, and although she was disappointed when her cousin declared herself too bored with the whole matter to give her any more information about the trip she was to take, she agreed readily enough to wait until Sister Brewster had been informed of the change. "She'll send for you," laughed Hilary, "and fuss and fret about a hundred and one things, but you don't need to take any notice, love – I can't think what Lady Marchant was about, suggesting that old Brewster should be in charge."

"How many children?" asked Arabella.

Hilary shrugged. "Do you know, I can't remember – not many, though, most of them . . ." she stopped abruptly and made some remark about the traffic, so that the sentence never got finished.

Wickham's looked as grey and forbidding as it always did, even on a lovely autumn day, its brick walls and rows of windows looked uninviting, and now, today, under a pale sky with a threat of rain, and a wind blowing the first of the leaves from the row of plane trees across the London square, it looked more inhospitable than ever. But Arabella didn't notice, and if she had, she wouldn't have minded; she was happy at Wickham's – in a year's time, when she had finished her training, she would probably take a job in some other hospital, but that was a long while yet. She parked the car in the corrugated iron shed set apart for the nursing staff and walked with her cousin to the side entrance which would take them to the Nurses' Home. She had barely half an hour before she was due on duty; she bade Hilary a swift goodbye and raced along the complexity of passages which would get her to the Home.

On the third floor, where she had her room, there was a good deal of laughing and talking. Second dinner was just over, the young ladies who had eaten it were making themselves a cup of tea. They crowded into her room, obligingly filling a mug of the comforting liquid for her, and carrying on a ceaseless chatter while she cast off her green jersey dress and tore into her blue and white striped uniform. Between heartening mouthfuls of scalding tea, she answered her companions' questions as to her days off, exclaimed suitably over the latest hospital gossip, and agreed to go with a number of her friends to the cinema on her next free evening. It wasn't until they were crowding through the door that she told them she was going to take her cousin's place on the children's bus trip.

The dozen or so nurses milling around her paused in their headlong flight back to their work on the wards. "Arabella, you can't!" exclaimed Anne Morgan, one of her particular friends. "Old Brewster's in charge and there are to be twenty-two kids and they're almost all more or less helpless – it'll be terrible!"

"Why can't your cousin go?" a voice wanted to know.

Arabella got out of answering that one by exclaiming, "Lord, look at the time!" and belting down the stairs. Going on duty at two o'clock after days off was bad enough, it would be ten times worse if one were late and incurred the displeasure of the Ward Sister.

She slid into Women's Medical with thirty seconds to spare, and when Sister came through the door a minute later, Arabella was making up an empty bed for all the world as though she had been at it for five minutes or more.

She had no time to herself after that, and when she went off duty that evening, her impending journey was quite overlooked in the scattered conversations carried on between baths and cups of tea and the trying on, by at least six of her closest friends, of a hat which had been delivered to Anne that evening. She was to be bridesmaid to her sister within a short time, and the hat was a romantic wide-brimmed affair, all ribbons and lace. It suited Anne very well – it suited them all, it was that kind of a hat, but when it was offered to Arabella she laughingly refused; her aunt had advised her that the maxim "A plain hat for a plain face," was a good one, and Arabella had faithfully abided by it. All the same, when she came back from her bath some twenty minutes later and found everyone gone and the hat on Anne's bed, she settled the masterpiece of millinery upon her head and looked rather fearfully in the mirror.

Aunt Maud had been wrong; the hat did something for her, she looked almost pretty. She winced at the memory of the severe felt she had purchased for church-going last winter, with her aunt's unqualified approval. The next hat she bought, she vowed, turning her head this way and that before the mirror, she would buy by herself, and it would be a hat to shock the family, the village churchgoers and the parson himself. She took it off with regret. It was a pity that as a general rule she didn't wear hats; all the same she glowed gently with the knowledge that she wasn't quite as plain as she had imagined. It would be nice, she thought sleepily, if you were wearing such a hat when Nanny's Mr. Right came along, if ever he came, which seemed unlikely.

Two days later Sister Brewster sent for her, to inform

her in tones of disapproval that since her cousin was unable to go on the children's holiday which Lady Marchant had so kindly arranged, and Matron had signified her approval of Arabella taking her place, she would have to make do with whoever was offered her. Upon this rather unfortunate opening she proceeded to build her plans for the expedition, merely pausing from time to time in order to tell Arabella that she was to do as she was told at all times. "I shall have my hands full," stated Sister Brewster loftily, "and I want no nonsense of any sort."

Arabella wondered if the programme — and a very muddled one it was too — was to be adhered to, what time there would be left for her to do more than draw breath, let alone give way to any sort of nonsense. She assured the older lady that she wasn't the nonsensical type, and then enquired how many children they were to escort.

"Twenty-two," said Sister Brewster snappily.

"Are they all able to help themselves?"

"Some ten or eleven are capable of doing most things. You will need to help the others."

Arabella caught her breath, clamped her teeth firmly on to her tongue and remained commendably silent. It was going to be far worse than she had been led to believe; no wonder Hilary hadn't wanted to go, although she might not have known the details when she cried off. Arabella, who wouldn't have played a dirty trick on anyone, couldn't imagine others doing so, especially her own cousin.

She went along to the Sisters' Wing of the Home that evening and told Hilary about it, and her cousin, sitting before her mirror, doing things to her pretty face, made a sympathetic sound. "Poor old Bella, I am sorry, love. Never mind, it won't be for long and once you get to the camp I'm sure you'll find swarms of volunteer helpers, then you won't have nearly so much to do."

She applied mascara with an expert hand and Arabella watched with an appreciative eye. "We're leaving in two days' time," she told her cousin. "Did you do anything about Watts' holiday?"

Hilary got up and put on her coat. "Watts? Don't worry your head, Bella – everything will be arranged."

Arabella prepared to leave. "Where are you going?" she inquired.

Hilary gave her a mischievous smile. "Just a little dinner for two. I'm late – be a darling and tidy up a bit for me, will you? I'll be late back and I know I'll be too tired... 'bye, love."

She was gone in a discreet cloud of Ma Griffe and Arabella started to put away discarded clothes and tidy the dressing table. She had done it before quite a number of times, and as she opened doors and closed drawers she reflected, without envy, that her cousin was certainly the prettiest girl she had ever seen. The thought sent her to the mirror to peer at her own reflection, an action so unrewarding that she made haste to go back to her own room.

Lady Marchant, even though she was in Canada, had seen to it that her work in arranging a holiday for the

21

spastic children should not go unsung; the children were conveyed to Wickham's in the morning where the bus was waiting for them, together with a battery of cameramen from all the best newspapers and even someone from the B.B.C.

Arabella, busy arranging the children in their most comfortable positions and then strapping them in, had no time to pose for her photograph, although she was assured by her friends later that there were some excellent shots of her back view on the six o'clock news, but Hilary, who had come down into the courtyard ostensibly to help, turned her lovely face to the cameramen, who realized that she was exactly what they were looking for. They snapped her in a dozen positions and the B.B.C. reporter managed a short interview, in which Hilary, without actually saying so, gave the impression that she was in charge of the whole excursion.

The bus left at length, half an hour after everyone else, because Sister Brewster, at the last minute, had discovered that she had left behind most of the papers she needed for the journey; it was unfortunate that she couldn't remember where she had left them. They came to light in her room finally, but by then the newspaper men and the reporter had gone home to their lunch.

Contrary to her expectations, Arabella enjoyed the journey; the children were good even though they were wild with excitement; most of them were able to do only a very little for themselves even though they had the intelligence of a normal child. Arabella listened patiently to their slow, difficult speech, pointed out the sights as

22

they went along, and when the bus pulled in to a layby, helped them to eat their lunches. Several of them needed to be fed, several more needed a steadying hand. It took so long that she ate her own sandwiches once the bus had started again, sitting up in front with three of the more helpless of the children. They were pathetically lightweight, so they were close to the driver and the bus door, so that they could be whisked in and out quickly and leave room for those not quite so handicapped. The driver, Arabella had quickly decided, was a dear; quite elderly and rather thickset, a good steady driver too and not easily distracted by the shouts and noise going on around him.

They were to cross by Hovercraft to Calais and spend the night near Ghent, at a convent known to Lady Marchant, and despite Sister Brewster's misgivings, the journey went smoothly and surprisingly rapidly. Once on the other side of the channel, Mr. Burns, the driver, took the coast road to Dunkirk, turning off there to cross into Belgium and so eventually to Ghent. The convent was just outside the town, a charming red brick building enclosed by a large garden and with a gratifyingly large number of helpers waiting to receive them. The children were fed and put to bed and the three of them were sitting down to their own supper in a commendably short space of time. They talked little, for they were tired, and Arabella for one was glad to stretch herself out in her severe little bed in the room allotted to her leading from the children's dormitory.

They were on their way directly after a breakfast

23

eaten at an hour which had meant getting up very early indeed, but the morning was fine if chilly and spirits were high as Mr. Burns turned the bus towards Holland. They had a journey of roughly a hundred and fifty miles to go and more than five hours in which to do it, for they were expected at the camp by one o'clock. Part of the journey at least would be on the motorway, the remainder as far as Arnhem on a first-class road. The holiday camp was nine or ten miles further on, in the Veluwe, and with no towns of any size nearby, that much Arabella had learned from her study of the map before they had left, and as they went along, Mr. Burns supplied odds and ends of information concerning the country around them.

They were through Arnhem and off the main road now, tooling along through pleasant quiet country, wooded and sparsely inhabited – a little like the New Forest, decided Arabella, on her way round the bus with sweets for the children. It was as she was making her way to the front again that she noticed that Mr. Burns' driving had become rather erratic; he wasn't on the right side of the road any more, but well in the middle. The bus shot back to the right far too sharply and then, as though propelled by some giant hand, to the left. Arabella was beside a strangely sagging Mr. Burns by now, applying the hand-brake, switching off the ignition and then leaning across his inert body to drag at the wheel. The bus came to a lop-sided halt on the wrong side of the road, on a narrow grass slope leading to a small waterway. It took a few long seconds to decide what it

24

would do next and then tilted sideways and slid slowly over. Arabella had ample time to see a car, coming fast and apparently straight at them. Her head was full of a jumble of thoughts, tilting themselves sideways out of her mind just as the bus was tilting – Sister Brewster, squeaking like a parrot; the children, gasping and crying incoherently for help; Hilary, telling her it would be quite an easy trip and she had nothing to worry about; last and most strangely, a vivid memory of Anne's gorgeous bridesmaid's hat.

The bus landed on its side quite gently and lay rocking. She heard the squeal of brakes as she tried to twist round to hold the children nearest to her upright.

CHAPTER TWO

THERE was someone trying to open the driver's door, now crazily above Arabella's head. She could hear a man's voice, uttering harsh foreign words as the door handle came away uselessly in his hand and fell within inches of her head. The next moment she saw a large hand slide through the partly opened glass top of the door and work its way to the inside handle; when the door opened with a protesting groan, the hand's owner put his head through and stared down at her.

He was a good-looking man, not so very young, with fair hair and blue eyes under thick arched brows. Arabella examined his face with a dreamlike detachment brought on through shock, but when he allowed his gaze to roam rapidly round the chaos around her, she pulled herself together.

"Please help us," she was glad to hear her voice was steady. "These children are spastics." Even as she spoke she wondered if he understood a word she said.

Apparently he did, for he disappeared without a word, leaving her a prey to the fear that he might have decided that it would be more prudent to get help rather than start rescue operations on his own. Her fears were groundless, however; she heard the door at the back of the bus being wrenched open with some difficulty and his voice, speaking English this time, telling Sister Brewster with firm authority to climb out into the road and stop any car which might come along. She couldn't hear Sister Brewster's reply, but the squawking had stopped.

The bus had stopped rocking by now, but there was water slopping through the half-open windows at the back. Arabella made shift to unbuckle two or three of the children who were getting wet, and lift them on to the other side of the bus, to sit them higgledy-piggledy on top of the children already there. She heard the man's voice again and saw that he was back, leaning precariously through the door. He spoke with approval:

"Good girl – move as many as you can from that side, but keep away from the back, the bus may slide even more. We'll get the children out in a minute or two, but first I must move the driver."

Arabella cried: "He's . . ." and stopped herself just in time because the children had stopped their wailing and crying to listen. "Isn't he?" she asked.

"Yes. Tell me the names of any of the children who can help themselves enough to get out of the back of the bus."

"John, Teddy, Peter . . ." she paused. "Sister Brewster's there," she reminded him.

"No use at the moment – go on."

"I can't remember any more names, but they can help William and Joan once they're out. They're not too good on their feet, but they could manage."

27

She could hear him telling them what to do; he had a deep, rather slow voice, it was very reassuring just listening to it; she felt her heartbeats slow as her first fright subsided. It was just a question of getting the children out. She contrived to turn once more and take a more detailed look at her small companions. Some of them had minor cuts and red patches which would be nasty bruises later on and they would all be badly shocked; she thought briefly and with regret of poor Mr. Burns and then lifted her head again as their rescuer spoke.

"You'll have to help, I'm afraid. Untwist his feet from the pedals, will you?"

He made the request in a matter-of-fact way which made it easier for her to do as he had bidden her. Poor Mr. Burns disappeared from view and the way was more or less clear for the children.

"I'm afraid you must heave them from below," said the man, "but there's bound to be a car along soon and then we'll have help – it's a quiet road, but not as quiet as all that." He peered down. "Strapped to their seats, are they? Let's start with the little one beside you and then you'll have more room to turn round."

It was a slow business, for the children were unable to help themselves, but Arabella, although small, was sturdy and possessed the gift of patience. She had just pushed ten-year-old Bobby Trent's frail body below the door so that the man could lean down and catch him by the arms, when she heard a car pull up. Without loosening his hold on the little boy, the man turned his head and shouted something, and Arabella heard an answering voice before the car started up again, its urgent roar fading quickly into the distance.

The man grinned down at her. "Gone for help," he told her briefly, "and there's help here besides."

He lifted Billy as though he had been made of feathers and disappeared with him, to reappear after a moment and climb through the door. The bus had been overcrowded before, what with its cockeyed seats and scattered luggage and terrified children. Now there was no room to move, for he was an immensely tall man and largely made. But they were not cramped for long; another man appeared above them and now the children were being passed swiftly upwards and out to safety. Arabella, with an eye to the men's speed, began at once to unbuckle the remaining children so that no time should be lost. It was a difficult task, for the children were frightened, making their helplessness even more marked. She soothed them as best she could and tried to control wildly waving arms and legs, wishing that Sister Brewster could pull herself together and give a hand, although probably she was busy with the children already rescued.

"Would it be easier to get the rest of the children out of the back door?" ventured Arabella.

Her companion didn't pause in his rescue operations. "No – the bus is beginning to tilt at that end; we don't want to shift the balance, it might make it more awkward."

She considered that nothing could be more awkward than their task at that moment, but she kept silent. It was hardly an occasion for conversation, and the men seemed to know exactly what they were doing.

There were only five children left when she heard several cars stop close by with a tremendous squealing of brakes. The man beside her had called to his helper above, who in his turn shouted down to whoever it was who had arrived, and a moment later a round, serious face, crowned by a peaked cap, appeared at the door above them. "Police," muttered Arabella, and redoubled her efforts with the incredible muddle Sally Perkins had got herself and her straps into. The owner of the face seemed to know the man in the bus, for he listened to what he had to say, nodded his head in agreement and disappeared again.

Arabella could hear the singsong warning of the ambulances now, and the thought flitted through her head that she hadn't the least idea of what was to happen to them all; presumably someone would arrange something – perhaps Sister Brewster? No, on second thoughts, old Brewster would be waiting for someone else to do it for her. The last child was heaved gently aloft, so that he could be lifted clear of the bus, and Arabella found herself clipped round her neat waist and held high, so that she could be lifted through the door too, to be deposited gently on the grass. She was barely on her feet when the two men joined her. The second man spoke no English, but he smiled kindly at her, dusted her down, said "O.K." and when she thanked him, shook her by the hand and made off after a brief word. She wondered if the man who had come to their rescue was going too; his car was close by – a Bentley, a silver-grey piece of elegance which stirred her to envy.

"We had better take a look at these children before they go to hospital," remarked her companion.

"Hospital?" she echoed stupidly.

"In Doesburg."

"In Doesburg?" repeated Arabella, still stupid, knowing she sounded like a bad Greek chorus and unable to do anything about it.

He smiled at her very kindly. "I imagine that the other lady is in charge?" and at her nod: "If you will tell me her name? I think I should speak to her, then we will have a quick look at everyone and get them settled as quickly as possible." He turned to go and then paused to add: "I'm a doctor, by the way."

He glanced at the huddle of small figures lying and sitting awkwardly on the grass verge, being tended by ambulance men and police, and then allowed his gaze to rest upon Arabella, who looked deplorable; her overall stained with heaven knew what, her hair hanging wispily around a far from clean face; her cap – the cap Sister Brewster had insisted that she should wear, with some vague idea that it would uphold the prestige of the British nurse abroad – crushed and dirtied by desperate little fingers, pulled askew by some unhappy child.

Arabella was in no state to mind her appearance; she was indeed unaware of the doctor's amused and critical eye. Relief was surging through her, because they were all out of the ruined bus and here was a doctor at hand to help the children. She declared with fervour: "Gosh, I

31

am glad!" and started at once on the difficult task of discovering which of the children, if any, was seriously hurt.

The doctor was back beside her within a few minutes. "Sister Brewster will go with those children who can help themselves a little – they're going to the hospital now. Do you mind staying and giving a hand here?"

She accompanied him from child to child as he examined each one, leaving her to put on an emergency dressing here and there before they were whisked away to an ambulance. On the whole, they had got off lightly; cuts and bruises and terror, and a nervous excitement which had caused the children's condition to be grossly exaggerated. Only Billy Trent and Sally Perkins had suffered serious injury, for they each had broken a leg. Surprisingly, they were quieter than the other children, possibly exhausted by fright and pain and bewilderment. The doctor muttered to himself as he made them as comfortable as possible in the last waiting ambulance. "Hop in," he ordered Arabella tersely, and the expression sounded strange in his correct English. "I'll go ahead in the car."

He banged the door on her as though the very sight annoyed him, but she forgot that at once in her efforts to keep Billy and Sally happy once the ambulance was on the move.

They turned off the road after a very few minutes, to go through heathland and woods, cross beneath two main roads after a mile or so, and enter a small, pleasant

32

town. The hospital was situated some way back from its main street, a fairly modern building at the end of a cul-de-sac lined with small old houses. Its courtyard was a hive of activity and from what Arabella could see from the ambulance windows, there was no lack of helpers. Several people detached themselves now and came hurrying to undo the ambulance doors and convey the children inside; Arabella was swept inside too, with a kindly nurse's hand firmly under her elbow. She had time to glimpse the silver-grey of the Bentley parked on one side of the small forecourt before she was borne through the doors into what was apparently the entrance hall. But they didn't stay here. The trolleys bearing the children were already turning down a short passage leading away from the hall, and Arabella, urged on with gentle insistence by her companion, trotted obediently after them. Casualty, she saw at once, quite a nice one too, but just now filled to capacity with spastic children. . . . She barely had time to glimpse Sister Brewster lying back with her eyes closed, when the doctor appeared from nowhere beside her.

"Keep with these two," he counselled her. "X-Ray first, and then probably the plaster room – they'll feel better about the whole thing if they see you around."

She nodded, and then remembered to voice a doubt at the back of her mind. "Mr. Burns – his people in England, and Wickham's – should someone do something?"

"It's being done now. Off to X-Ray – I must go and have another chat with Sister Brewster."

Arabella perceived that for the moment at any rate she was a nurse, not a young woman who had had a nasty fright and needed, above all things, a nice cup of tea and a good cry. She said quietly: "Yes, very well, doctor," and was brought to a halt by his: "She has brown hair, and speaks soft like a woman."

"*The Merry Wives of Windsor*," she stated automatically, and wondered if he had sustained an injury to his head while he was in the bus. It seemed not.

"The sight of you called it to mind," he explained, and walked away, leaving her to accompany Billy and Sally to X-Ray.

It took a long time to get everyone sorted out, especially as Sister Brewster, instead of being helpful and efficient, lay back and declared that she was far too poorly to be bothered with a lot of questions and plans. Arabella, freed for a short time from Billy and Sally while they were anaesthetized while their legs were put in plaster, drank the cup of coffee someone put into her hand and then helped get the remaining children into their beds.

The hospital had risen nobly to the occasion; extra beds were being put up, more staff had been called back on duty, there was a supply of night garments and a trolley of warm drinks and soup. Arabella, almost dropping with tiredness, her appearance more deplorable than ever and starving for food, toiled on. The children had rallied amazingly. They had all been examined by now; two house doctors and the doctor who had come to their help in the first place had checked each one of them carefully. There was nothing, they declared, that could not be put right by a good night's sleep and a day or two's rest before being sent home. Excepting for Sally and Billy, of course, who would have to stay for a week or two.

Sister Brewster had retired to bed in the Nurses' Home, tearfully contradicting herself with every breath and far more worried about a bruise on her arm than anything else. Arabella, called away from the children to speak to her superior, was put out to find that Sister Brewster didn't much care what happened to anybody but herself; she made no enquiries as to Arabella's state of mind or body, declared peevishly that Mr. Burns should never have been sent on the journey without a medical examination, and even implied that it was all his fault, which annoyed Arabella so much that she would have liked to have answered back, only she had a sudden urge to cry, and that would never have done. She wished Sister Brewster a cold good night instead and went back to the children, to help them eat their suppers and then go from bed to bed, tucking them in and kissing them in a motherly fashion.

She was on her way down to the hospital dining room with a friendly group of nurses, intent on her comfort, when a voice over the intercom requested, in good English, that the nurse who had accompanied the children should present herself at Doctor van der Vorst's office. "The younger of the two nurses," added the voice.

"Who's he?" demanded Arabella of those around her, a little cross because her thoughts were bent on supper and bed. She neither knew nor cared for the moment what arrangements had been made nor who was making them. Presumably someone would sort everything out and they would all be sent home, but now all that she wanted was food and a good sleep so that she could forget Mr. Burns, dying with such awful suddenness, and the children's terrified little faces – she had been terrified herself.

No one had taken any notice of her question, perhaps they hadn't understood, but she had been led down a short passage and stood before a door upon which several helpful knuckles rapped before opening it and pushing her gently inside.

Doctor van der Vorst looked quite different, sitting at a large desk piled most untidily with a variety of papers, but the look he gave her was the same calm, friendly one which had cheered her when she had peered up in that awful bus and seen him staring down at her. He got up as she took a few steps into the room and said: "Hullo – I do apologise for taking up your time, you have been working for two since you got here, so I'm told, you must be asleep on your feet. But I must have some particulars, and unfortunately Sister Brewster doesn't feel able to help."

He paused, waiting for her comment, no doubt, but Arabella, much as she disliked old Brewster, was loyal. "She's very shocked," she offered in her pleasant voice, a little roughened because she was so tired, and took the chair he offered her, facing him across the desk. The door behind her opened and a homely body, very clean and starched, came in with a tray.

"Coffee?" enquired the doctor. "It will keep you going until you can get to your supper."

The coffee was hot and milky and sweet, and there were little sandwiches besides. Arabella gobbled delicately and when she had drunk her coffee and her cup had been filled again, the doctor spoke.

"I've done what I could," he began in his slow, pleasant voice. "I've telephoned your hospital, who are dealing with notifying relatives and so forth, attended to the matter of Mr. Burns and made a preliminary list of the children's names, but not yours. . . ." He paused, his eyebrows raised in enquiry and Arabella, whisking the last delicious crumb into her mouth with a pink tongue, made haste to tell him: "Arabella Birch."

He scribbled. "You are a nurse at Wickham's Hospital?"

She nodded. "I've still a year's training to do before I take my Finals, but I'm children's trained." And because he still looked enquiring, she went on: "I'm twenty-two and I live with my aunt and uncle when I'm not in hospital. Mr. and Mrs. Birch at Little Dean House, Little Sampford, Essex."

"There is a telephone number?"

She gave that too and he picked up the receiver beside him and spoke into it, then turned to the papers before him. "Will you check these names with me?" He hardly glanced at her, but began to read down the list in front of him, a slow business, for she had to correct him several times, give the children's ages and the extent of their disability and any other details she could remember. They were almost at the end when the telephone rang once more. "They are getting your home," he told her, "and will ring back. I expect you would like to speak to your family."

"Oh, yes – you're very k-kind. I'm sure Wickham's w-will have t-telephoned, but that's not the s-same ..." she added suddenly. "P-poor Mr. Burns!"

The doctor stared at her across his desk. "I telephoned his wife a little while ago – I too am deeply sorry. Shall we get on with this list?"

It was complete by the time the telephone rang again. The doctor grunted something into the receiver and pushed the instrument towards her.

"Don't worry," he told her, and smiled nicely as he went out of the room. Just the sort of man, thought Arabella, watching him go, one would wish to have with one in a tight corner – quite unflappable, and knowing what to do about everything. She picked up the receiver and waited patiently until her aunt's excited voice had calmed a little before embarking on the skeleton of their day's adventure. When she had finished her aunt said: "You're coming back home, of course, Arabella – your uncle will come down and meet you. ..."

Her heart warmed to this unexpected kindness. "That's very sweet of him, b-but I d-don't know ... I should think the ch-children would be travelling b-back in a d-day or so, but I don't know how, and there are t-two of them who will have to stay – they both have f-fractures. I'll t-telephone you as soon as I know."

She said goodbye then and sat quietly in her chair, waiting for the doctor to come back. It was peaceful in the room, and in an austere way, pleasant too; there were a quantity of bookshelves stuffed with heavy tomes, a gently ticking clock on the wall and thick blue curtains drawn across the tall windows. The walls were hung with portraits of wise-looking gentlemen whom Arabella took to be previous governors and members of the medical profession attached to the hospital – the one behind the desk was particularly severe; she closed her eyes to avoid his pointed stare and went to sleep.

She wakened within minutes to find the doctor standing over her.

"I'm s-so s-sorry," she began, and was annoyed to find that her stammer, which hadn't been too much in evidence, had returned. "I was t-trying not t-to look at th-that m-man over there."

"My great-grandfather," remarked the doctor briefly. "You're tired out, we'll talk again in the morning – there are still several things . . ." He smiled suddenly. "Sleep after toil, port after stormy seas – I must say you look as though you've come through stormy seas and you have certainly toiled."

She ignored the last part of his remark, but: "Spenser," she confirmed, "isn't it from the *Faerie Queen*?"

He nodded as she got to her feet. "I don't feel that I have anything in common with someone as delicate and dainty as that," she said soberly, and he laughed again.

"No? I daresay I shan't recognise you in the morning, you will look so prim and neat." he opened the door. "Goodnight, Arabella."

There was a nurse hovering outside, waiting for her, a large, friendly girl, who sat with her while she ate her supper and then took her upstairs to a small, nicely furnished room where the bed had been invitingly turned down and someone had thoughtfully arranged a nightie, a brush and comb and a toothbrush on a chair.

Arabella looked with horror at her appearance in the mirror, had a bath, brushed her hair in a perfunctory fashion and jumped into bed, considerably hampered by the nightie, which was a great deal too large. She was asleep within seconds of laying her head on the pillow.

She felt quite herself in the morning, for she was young and strong, and besides had learned from an early age to school her feelings; giving way to these had been something her uncle had discouraged; he never gave way to his, and although Hilary and her mother were allowed to be the exception to his rule, everyone else about him was expected to be what he described as sensible. So Arabella wasted no time in self-pity but dressed in the clean overall someone had found for her, pinned a borrowed cap upon her now very neat head, and when a nurse knocked on the door and asked if she were ready for breakfast, declared cheerfully that she was.

Not that she thought much of the meal; bread and butter and cheese and jam seemed a poor exchange after Wickham's porridge and bacon, but the coffee was delicious and everyone was very kind, chattering away to her in sketchy English and occasionally, when they forgot, in Dutch. And they were quick to help, for when she asked if she might see Sister Brewster, she was taken at once to that lady's room, to find her sitting up in bed with a tray before her.

"I feel very poorly," declared Sister Brewster as soon as Arabella entered the room. "I have hardly closed my eyes all night and I have a shocking headache. I shall be glad to get back to Wickham's and have a few days off in which to recover, for I have had a great shock."

Arabella let this pass and waited for her to enquire about the children, or for that matter, about herself, but when the older woman remained silent she said: "Well, if you don't mind, Sister, I'm going to the ward to see how the children are."

Her companion shot her a baleful look. "I can see that this dreadful experience has hardly touched you," she commented sourly. "I suppose you found it all very exciting."

"No," said Arabella patiently, "I didn't find it at all exciting when Mr. Burns died, nor when the children were hurt and frightened. Do you want anything before I go, Sister?"

"No," her superior sounded pettish, "you'll have to see to everything. I'm in no fit state to cope with anything – my head."

Arabella bit back some naughty remarks about her companion's head and went out, closing the door smartly behind her.

She received a quite different welcome from the children. True, they had bruises and cuts and one or two

41

black eyes, but they were smiling again, trying to express themselves as they had their breakfast. Arabella went to feed Sally and Billy, lying side by side in their beds and inclined to be grizzly and saw with surprise that Doctor van der Vorst was already doing a ward round, going from child to child with a couple of young doctors and the Ward Sister. When he reached Arabella he stopped, wished her good morning and wanted to know how she felt.

"F-fine, thank you, Doctor," said Arabella, annoyed about the stammer.

"Good. Will you come to the office at eleven o'clock, Nurse Birch? I – er – gather that Sister Brewster is still confined to her bed."

"Her head aches," said Arabella flatly.

He nodded again. "In that case, we must endeavour to make all the necessary arrangements without bothering her unduly, must we not?" he asked smoothly as he bent to examine the two children. "These fractures are in good alignment; they should do well." He smiled at Billy and Sally, ruffled their hair, made a little joke so that they smiled at last, and passed on to the next bed.

He wasn't sitting at his desk when she entered the office later on, but standing at the window, looking out, but he turned to her with a smile and came forward to pull out a chair for her.

"How I do take up your time," he remarked pleasantly, "but I feel we must get these children back home as soon as possible, don't you agree? The camp to which you were going is quite unsuitable for them, I'm afraid, for most of them are still shocked, not to mention bruises and cuts; to go back to their own familiar surroundings and people they know and trust is essential. I've been on the telephone this morning and we have arranged to fly them back the day after tomorrow – I'll engage to have ambulances to take them to Schiphol, and the staff there have promised their fullest co-operation The children will be met at London Airport – Wickham's will send nurses and ambulances and give them another check-up before they go to their homes." He paused. "I have just been visiting Sister Brewster, who feels that she is well enough to accompany them," his voice was dry. "There remains the question of Sally and Billy; it is out of the question that they should leave the hospital for the moment. I suggest that you should remain here with them, Arabella."

She saw her holiday with Doreen fading to a regretful oblivion. Doreen couldn't be expected to change her holidays yet again – besides, by the time she got back to England it would be October and she couldn't expect her friend to miss the last of the autumn weather. A wild idea that Hilary might come out in her place crossed her mind, to be instantly dismissed. Mr. Thisby-Barnes, for the moment at any rate, was far too important a factor in her cousin's life. She said slowly:

"If you s-say so, d-doctor, and if Wickham's d-doesn't mind."

He smiled at her. "Apparently not. It was suggested to the Matron – by your cousin, I believe – is she not a Ward Sister at Wickham's?"

43

"Yes. Who is to tell Sally and Billy?"

"You, Arabella; they trust you, don't they, and you'll know just what to say. They have homes? They aren't orphans?"

She racked her brains for the information she had primed herself with before she had started on the ill-fated trip. "No, they come from good homes, I believe, but poor, though. I'm sure their mothers and fathers came to see them off."

"I'll see if we can arrange something." He sounded vague. "You don't mind staying?"

It wouldn't be much use saying that she did, she concluded ruefully.

"Not at all," she spoke with such politeness that he shot her a keen glance before going on to say:

"Good – if you would be kind enough to look after the two of them – day duty, of course, and the usual off-duty hours. I think it might be best if we paid you as though you were a member of our own nursing staff, and any adjustments can be made when you get back. Have you sufficient money for the moment?"

"Yes, thank you – the police gave me my handbag and case."

He stood up. "I won't keep you any longer." He went to the door to open it for her. "I am grateful to you for your help."

She paused by him, looking up into his face; he wasn't only a very handsome man, he was kind too, even though she perceived that he was in the habit of getting his own way. "Who are you?" she asked.

A little smile tugged at the corner of his mouth. "I have a practice in the town," he told her, "and I am Medical Director of this hospital."

"How fortunate it was that you should have come along."

"A happy accident, shall we say, Arabella, if one might use the term without giving offence. You don't mind if I call you Arabella?"

The stammer, which had been happily absent, came back with a rush.

"N-no, n-not in the l-least." In fact she liked to be called Arabella by him, but it would never do to say so; she liked him very much, but he was still the Medical Director, being kind to a strange nurse who had been forced, willy-nilly through circumstances, to join his staff. To be on the safe side, she added "sir."

CHAPTER THREE

ARABELLA found that she slipped into the Dutch hospital's routine easily enough. True, there were difficulties with the language, which she considered quite outlandish and impossible to pronounce, but a great number of the staff spoke a little English; the house doctors spoke it fluently, so, more or less, did the Directrice, a large, bony woman with the face of a good-tempered horse and the disposition of an angel. It was she who explained to Arabella about her off-duty and her days off, and what would be expected of her when she was on duty; mostly the care of the two spastic children who were injured, she discovered, and when they didn't need her attention, help with the routine ward duties.

For the first two days she was kept busy, for Sister Brewster, although feeling better, seemed to think that it was beneath her dignity to come on to the wards and help with her little charges. She contented herself with twice-daily consultations with Arabella, during which she uttered a great many statements, each one contradicting the last; never ceased to lament their misfortunes, and shook her head doubtfully over Doctor van der Vorst's decision to keep Arabella at the hospital to look after Billy and Sally. But she was far too anxious to get home to trouble overmuch about this, beyond warning Arabella to remember that she was still only a student nurse even if she had her Children's training. Arabella listened meekly, for there was nothing much she could do about it, although she felt ashamed of Sister Brewster with her whining voice, looking on the black side of everything.

It could have been so much worse; the children could have been seriously injured, even killed. Doctor van der Vorst might never have come along that particular road at that particular time. Arabella considered that they had a great deal to be thankful for, but it would have been useless to say so; she could see that Sister Brewster, now that she was on the point of departure, was about to shed her role of a woman battered by cruel fate and a number of children who could do nothing much for themselves, and assume a quite different part in their adventure. Arabella guessed that she would have a quite different tale to tell by the time she reached Wickham's.

In this she was quite correct, but she was unaware that Doctor van der Vorst had already told the authorities at Wickham's his version of the whole affair, both by telephone and also in a remarkably concise letter, written in beautiful English. Not that Arabella minded over-much what Sister Brewster might fabricate when she returned; her own friends wouldn't believe a word of it, and old Brewster was noted for evading responsibility and laying the blame on other shoulders when anything went wrong.

So it was with faintly guilty pleasure that Arabella waved goodbye to the home-going party, setting off in their convoy of ambulances; it would be super not to have Sister Brewster's disapproving lectures twice a day; super to see something of the town and perhaps, if she were lucky, the surrounding countryside, super too, to accept the invitations extended to her by various members of the hospital staff to go to the local cinema with them, or shopping. She skipped happily up the staircase leading to the ward where Sally and Billy were being nursed. There was a cheerful hubbub of sound coming from behind its closed doors and no one to be seen, Arabella, feeling for some reason she didn't bother to question, delighted with life and the immediate future, started to whistle the first tune which came into her head: "Blow, blow, thou winter wind . . ." She rendered it happily if inappropriately, and then quite carried away, started to sing: "Thou art not so unkind . . ." slightly off key and regrettably loud. "As man's ingratitude . . ." She reached the top of the staircase and became aware all of a sudden that Doctor van der Vorst was beside her; he must have followed her silently up the stairs and what with the cheerful din from the ward and her noisy singing . . . She frowned fiercely, went a faint pink and said reprovingly :

"You made m-me jump! "

He had stopped in the short corridor before the ward doors and put out a long arm so that she was forced to stop too.

"I'm sorry – I was listening to your song – surely a little melancholy? Or do you perhaps feel that – er – man's ingratitude is indeed cold?"

She gave him a bright, candid look from hazel eyes,

which, while neither large nor brilliant, had a gentle beauty of their own.

"Of course not; everyone's been marvellous – just think, the whole hospital turned topsy-turvey for us – and nothing but kindness. I was singing because I feel happy."

His look told her that he understood what she meant. "I'm glad. We should all like you to enjoy your stay here. You must get out a little and see as much as possible. Arnhem is not too far away; there is a great deal to see there and the country around Doesburg is charming."

Arabella nodded, happily aware that for some reason, she wasn't stammering: "I should like that. It seems hardly fair, though, that I'm the only one who came on the trip to get any fun out of it."

"I should hardly consider working a full day on the children's ward to be fun," he remarked mildly.

"I get off-duty, and days off. How long do you think I shall be here, Doctor?"

"A few weeks, shall we say? perhaps less than that. Tell me, do Sally and Billy live at home all the time – do they not go to the Spastic Centre or somewhere similar?"

Arabella wrinkled her brow, trying to remember. "I think they went once or twice a week, but most of the children lived at home, you know – that's why Lady Marchant arranged this trip, so that they could see something of the world and give their families a short break."

He smiled faintly. "Very commendable. So the sooner

we get them away from hospital the better for them." He was leaning against the corridor wall, taking up a great deal of room, so that she couldn't go into the ward without squeezing past him. "We don't want them to fret."

For some reason this speech depressed Arabella, although she was sensible enough to see that they could be nothing but a nuisance while they remained at the hospital – taking up beds, and because of their affliction, requiring a good deal of attention. No wonder he wanted to be rid of them. She observed in a stiff voice: "There's no reason why they shouldn't go very soon, is there? They're both in plaster, and it isn't a very long journey."

He answered her gravely, although she had the impression that he was laughing at her. "It was not my intention to send them home at the moment. We'll see."

Arabella's silky brows knitted in another frown. See what? she pondered crossly. How infuriating it was when people said they would see without giving anyone else a clue as to what it was. She shot him a baffled look and found his gaze bent upon her so intently that she supposed a little impatiently that her hair was coming down or something of the sort.

"Don't let me keep you from your work," he begged her in a voice whose formality forced her to murmur meekly. He opened the ward door and she went past him with a muttered thank-you, feeling, after her short bout of high spirits, depressed and irritable.

She saw very little of the doctor for the next two or three days, only when he went round the hospital with whichever doctor was on duty, hedged in, just as the senior doctors and surgeons at Wickham's, by the Ward Sister, the Social Worker, the Path Lab people and someone from Physio. True, he was punctilious in his enquiries as to her comfort, but only after he had required a detailed account of Billy and Sally and the progress they were making. The children were, in fact, doing very well, and now that they had become accustomed to the new faces around them and understood that if Arabella went off duty she would be back again and wasn't leaving them for good, they were increasingly easy to look after. She had them up now, strapped into wheeled chairs, taking them round the wards and out into the garden at the back of the hospital and spending a great deal of time over their speech therapy. Billy fed himself after a fashion, Sally was still struggling to do so; it needed infinite patience and good humour to care for them, but Arabella, possessing both these attributes, made light of the messy mealtimes and the minutes wasted while one or other of the two children strove to say what an intelligent little brain wished to convey to her, and was largely prevented.

The party in the care of Sister Brewster had been safely home for several days when Arabella was called to Doctor van der Vorst's office. When she knocked and went in he got up from his desk and said briskly:

"I should have come in search of you, but I am waiting for a telephone call and as I must refer to a pile of notes, I didn't dare to go from the room. Sit down, won't you? Are you quite happy about Sally and Billy?"

Arabella said that yes, thank you, she was, and sat silent, studying him. He was extremely handsome, she acknowledged, and although he was so large, he wasn't clumsy with it. She liked the way his hair grew from a high forehead, and his kind mouth and determined chin. The eyebrows were expressive, and presumably if he were in a temper, could be quite terrifying, and even if his nose were a thought too large his eyes were nice. . . . She became aware that she had been staring and looked away quickly as he glanced up from the papers before him.

"I thought you might like to know that I've heard from Wickham's," he observed blandly. He glanced at a letter on his desk. "A Doctor Forster, who assures me that you are eminently suitable to look after Sally and Billy. He suggests that he leaves it to me to decide when it is possible for them to travel back to England, and asks that you remain with them and escort them when they go. I hope you will agree to do this?"

She beamed with pleasure and his rather formal manner melted into a smile of great charm.

"Well, of c-course I'll s-stay. I t-told you the other d-day that I liked b-being here." A little tardily, she added, "Doctor."

"I should like, if I may, to try a little experiment," he went on smoothly, just as though she hadn't said a word, "with the children – for I believe that they will improve a good deal more quickly if they are not in hospital. I propose to take them to my home and see how they react to more informal surroundings. That would necessitate you coming with them, if you have no objection."

She had no objection at all, in fact the idea filled her with a pleasant excitement. It would be interesting to see what sort of a home he had; she felt sure that he was married and probably had children of his own. A vague, half realized thought formed at the back of her head that if ever she were to marry, her husband would have to be just such a man as he. Perhaps he was a little old – at least thirty-five, she judged, but that wouldn't matter. She collected her wandering wits with something of an effort and asked: "When do you want to take them?"

"You have a day off tomorrow, would you come with me to my home? It would seem advisable for you not to be a complete stranger to it when you bring the children. Shall we say half past ten tomorrow morning? We can discuss which day they should come, then?"

He hadn't waited to see if she had any plans, had he? she reflected vexedly – now, if she had been Hilary, he wouldn't have been quite so high-handed; one at least of the doctors in the hospital would have dated her for her days off, probably she wouldn't have had a spare moment for weeks ahead. She thought soberly that to be a plain girl had no advantages at all, and how mortifying it was that he should be so certain that she had nothing better to do with her free time. Her voice was tart and the stammer was worse than ever. "I'm n-not s-sure if half p-past t-ten. . . ."

He interrupted so smoothly that she scarcely noticed it. "Thoughtless of me – you have made a number of friends already, haven't you? I'll fix another day when you're on duty." His voice was blandly friendly. "It's hardly fair of me to trespass on your free time."

Honesty and a desire to allow him to think that she was being sought after by every member of his staff warred within her. Honesty won.

"I was only going shopping with Zuster Marksma. She's on duty again at lunchtime, so she said she would show me where I could catch the bus to Arnhem. There's an open-air museum there."

The doctor received this widely known piece of information without even the ghost of a smile. He said composedly: "Then I am lucky. So shall we say half past ten?"

Arabella nodded. "Yes, thank you. I could catch the bus afterwards, couldn't I?"

He looked at her with a serious face, but his eyes were alight with laughter. "Certainly, if you wish."

He got up and opened the door for her and as she went past him, laid a large hand on her shoulder. "Thank you, Arabella," said the doctor, and just for a moment she thought he was going to say something more, but all he did was to incline his head gravely.

Arabella had few clothes with her, for at the camp she would have been busy with the children for most of the day. She had packed a skirt and some thin sweaters as well as her duty clothes, and at the last minute had flung in a jersey dress of honey and cinnamon stripes. She had had no notion of wearing it when she had packed it, but now, reviewing her scanty wardrobe, she was glad to have it with her. She did her face with great care, took a long time over her neatly piled hair, and viewed the result with mixed feelings, seeing, as always, the brilliant image of Hilary beside her in the mirror. She sighed as she caught up the sensible fawn-coloured raincoat her aunt had advised her to buy. "Something practical, dear," Aunt May had suggested kindly, "for you must never forget that although your home is and always will be with your uncle and me, you will have to manage on your own – with money, I mean." She had cast a contemptuous glance at the gaily coloured affairs Arabella had been looking at. "These are perfectly all right for a girl who doesn't have to think too much of her future, but take my advice, Arabella, and buy something sensible which you will still be wearing in five years' time."

It was only two years since her aunt had said that and she had taken her advice, albeit reluctantly, and already she hated the garment. The prospect of having to wear it for another three years or more filled her with loathing. As she went through the Home to the hospital entrance, Arabella toyed with the idea of buying some new clothes while she was in Holland – the sort of clothes she had always wanted, the clothes, came the unbidden thought, instantly suppressed, that Hilary wore. The idea animated her expression so that her eyes sparkled and her generous mouth curved into a pleased smile. She bounced past Piet, the head porter, wishing him a cheerful good morning as she went, and out into the hospital forecourt, quite unaware that she looked quite pretty.

Doctor van der Vorst was already there, leaning on the bonnet of the Bentley with a careless negligence which seemed to Arabella to be nothing short of sacrilege; the Bentley was almost new and its gleaming, pristine dignity required nothing short of the greatest respect.

She wished him good morning and spoke her thought. "You shouldn't lean against such a super car," she admonished him. "Supposing you should scratch it?"

He opened the door for her, laughing. "Then I should have to get another car, should I not?" He got in beside her. "How prompt you are – I supposed all girls never to be on time for a date."

She gave him one of her candid looks. "Well, this isn't a d-date, is it?"

He had turned the car and was going gently down the town's main street. "In the line of duty?" he wanted to know.

"Well, no, not that either. It's all right for me, because it's my day off, but you must have heaps to do . . ."

"No," the doctor contradicted her mildly, "it's my day off too."

She sat beside him, her thoughts very clearly to be read upon her expressive face. If he had a day off, would it be easy for her to leave as soon as she intended? She had visualised half and hour's quick inspection, a short discussion as to the best way of dealing with Billy and Sally in strange surroundings, a quick introduction to his wife and then she would make her goodbyes, while he would go back to whatever he chose to do with his free time. She had even prepared a little speech to this effect; now she would have to alter it. Perhaps too, if she mentioned the bus to Arnhem he might feel impelled to offer her a lift there; he had nice manners and he might insist. She began to think where she might go in that city so that if he insisted upon taking her there, she wouldn't have to hesitate as to where she wanted to go – she should never have mentioned her plans, but perhaps she would be able to slip away gracefully with a muttered excuse like people did in books.

"Don't worry about it," her companion begged, so suddenly that she jumped and with the stammer worse than ever assured him over-eagerly that she wasn't worried about anything.

He had left the main street now and turned into a tree-lined road where the houses, large and standing in their own grounds, stood well back from the pavement. There was a canal beside the road and on its other side, open fields and wooded country. Even on the rather grey morning, it looked delightful – a pleasant place to live in, Arabella conceded, talking silently to herself as usual, and was agreeably surprised when her companion turned the car once more between high, old-fashioned wrought iron gates, and up a drive, short and well gravelled, to halt silently before the double door set in the exact centre of a brick house, whose flat face rose three stories to a gabled roof. The house was of some size, with its rows of windows, all exactly alike, so that its placid face seemed to reflect the quiet countryside before it. Arabella got out when the doctor opened the car door and saw that the house door had been opened by an elderly woman in a black dress covered by an old-fashioned print apron. Her craggy face broke into a smile and she addressed herself to the doctor, who answered her briefly, and then said in English: "Our housekeeper, Emma, and our guardian angel, for Larissa never worries her head about household affairs."

He sounded fondly indulgent; so his wife was some beautiful helpless girl who couldn't cook a meal and doubtless didn't want to, let alone dust. Arabella was already disliking the mythical lady as she stepped over the threshold of the doctor's house, returning the housekeeper's warm smile with a shy one of her own.

She was allowed little time to look around her; she had a confused but pleasant impression of white walls and a flagstoned floor strewn with rugs, flowers in profusion, and dark polished furniture before the doctor opened one of the doors in the hall and ushered her into a large room at the front of the house. A tall, fair girl got up from one of the comfortable armchairs arranged around an enormous hooded chimneypiece and walked towards them, smiling. She was, Arabella saw with a jaundiced eye, much prettier than even her imagination had painted her, and her clothes were super.

"Hullo, Larissa," said the doctor cheerfully. "Here's Arabella." He turned to his visitor. "My sister, Larissa."

Arabella held out her hand and said in an astonished voice, "Oh. . . ." which prompted Larissa to ask: "Do I surprise you? Has Gideon been telling you tales about me?"

"No," said Arabella, "I didn't know . . . that is, I th-thought you were his w-wife."

His sister laughed. "Gideon? Why, he's a confirmed bachelor! Come and sit down, I have been hearing about your unfortunate journey – all those poor children – but also I hear that you are a very sensible and quick-thinking person. I am only just back home, or I should have come to the hospital to visit you all, but now there are only two children left, Gideon tells me, and you to nurse them . . ." She rattled on as she poured the coffee, which gave Arabella a good opportunity to study her. She was indeed a very pretty girl; her brother's good looks softened into near-beauty, and possessing an elegant figure which was set off to perfection by the clothes she was wearing. Arabella made polite conversation, sipped her delicious coffee and wished with all her heart that she could look just like that. She heaved a sigh, and looked up to find the doctor's gaze bent upon her, which made her colour guiltily, and prepared to embark upon some remark or other in case he might think her rude, staring in such a fashion. Happily there was no need of this, for there was a gentle, insistent barking at the door and when Doctor van der Vorst went to open it, an Old English sheepdog bounded in. He exchanged fulsome greetings with his master, gave Larissa a friendly nudge with his woolly head and went to sniff at Arabella, who flung an arm around him and begged to know his name.

"George," said the doctor, and the beast, hearing his name spoken by his master's voice, went to loll against his knees, his eyes cast up into his face with every appearance of bliss.

"Do the children like dogs?" Larissa asked.

"I hope so – though I don't really know. They're both

intelligent children, though, and very interested in everything."

"Good. We have two cats as well – come over here and see them."

They were in a corner of the room in a large box; a splendid Siamese whom Larissa introduced as Crosby, a small tabby cat with no pedigree whatsoever called Tatters, because, it was explained, Gideon had found her abandoned and brought her home one winter's night, and a quantity of kittens, all of them a curious mixture of tabby and Siamese.

"Ducky, aren't they?" asked Larissa, "and so devoted. Crosby adores Tatters and he's such a good father. They come in here during the day," she explained seriously, "but if I'm out they go into Gideon's study with him, or into the kitchen with Emma. They like company."

"They're beautiful!" exclaimed Arabella, and put a gentle finger on Tatters' commonplace head. "You wouldn't think that Crosby would fall for such an ordinary little thing, would you? I daresay she has a charming disposition, though."

"Indeed she has – I imagine the two children will love her." She turned to say to Gideon, "Shall I take Arabella to see the room we think might suit?"

The doctor got to his feet. "By all means, then if there is anything she wants altered it can be done before they arrive."

Arabella walked between them to the door. She would have liked the leisure to have looked around her, for there was a great deal meriting her inspection; paintings on the panelled walls, silver in a bow-fronted display cabinet, glass and china. . . . She said now, desperately anxious not to be a nuisance to the doctor: "But surely just for an hour or two, there'll be n-no n-need to alter. . . . Oh, I see, they're a b-bit messy with their m-meals, aren't they, and other things. . . . We could have our lunch in the garden, you know, for it's not in the least cold."

Larissa stopped short in the middle of the hall. "But didn't Gideon tell you?" she wanted to know. "You're coming to stay; he thinks it would be good for the children, and you're coming with them, of course."

Arabella looked at the doctor. "Well," she remarked reproachfully, "you never said a word – I thought you meant for a few hours."

He had halted too, standing under the portrait of a stern gentleman in a tie wig, who looked as though he might disagree with everything anyone might say. "Didn't I make myself clear? My apologies, dear girl, but what would be the use of a few hours – a day, even? We will have them here for a week or so, so that they may forget about the accident and the hospital and return home quite restored. I hear from Wickham's that they are having difficulty with some of the children; the experience seems to have shaken them more than we thought."

"Oh, I'm sorry to hear that," cried Arabella. "They try so hard, and when there's an improvement they're so pleased with themselves."

She hesitated and then asked diffidently: "Isn't it putting you to a great deal of inconvenience?"

"No," he answered coolly, "why should it? You will be here."

She felt snubbed. She replied in an expressionless voice: "Yes, of course."

The room they had gone to inspect was a large one at the back of the house, which, behind its flat façade, rambled a good deal. It had doors leading out to the garden, a small cloakroom conveniently close by, and another, much smaller room leading from it, which the doctor pointed out, would do very well for her. "But don't suppose that we intend to keep you all here like prisoners. I think that breakfast together would be a splendid idea. I'm usually home for lunch at midday. If I am not, Larissa will be; we can stow the children in the car and run them round and I've arranged for Emma's niece to relieve you for an hour or so each day. Perhaps not ideal, but worth a trial." He smiled at her. "What do you think?"

"It's a wonderful idea, but are you s-sure you d-don't mind?" She stopped to choose her words carefully. "They're n-not very easy to have around, you know." She gave him a questioning look and he said quickly: "We don't mind," in a reassuring voice, but she was not quite convinced.

"They're not – they can't help b-being careless s-sometimes," she persisted. "They might s-spoil things." Her eyes took in the extreme comfort of the room.

"Very unlikely," the doctor said bracingly. "This

house and its contents have stood up to countless generations of children banging and thumping around and dropping things all over it. Don't worry.

He took her arm, and with Larissa on the other side, walked her through the French window into the garden; a pleasant place, well shielded by trees so that no other house could be seen, and with a wide stretch of lawn beneath them, besides flower beds full of autumn flowers. George padded softly beside them as they wandered down the path to a wicket gate set in a high wall. "The kitchen garden," explained Larissa. "I'm a rotten gardener, but Gideon loves to dig and cut the grass, though we have Jaap to work here as well. Have you a garden at your home?"

Without realizing that she was doing so, Arabella told them both a good deal about herself, gently led by the casual questions put to her by the doctor, only she didn't say much about Hilary; the doctor wasn't likely to meet her cousin, and Arabella wasn't sure why she was deliberately reticent on the subject, although she felt mean about it.

They had come in from the garden by now, back into the sitting room, and Arabella, with an astonished look at the clock, said rather awkwardly: "I've stayed too long. I do b-beg your p-pardon, and I've such a lot to do."

She got to her feet, feeling she had excused herself rather gracefully, and was shattered by the doctor's abrupt: "What?" She stared at him and he repeated patiently: "You said that you had a lot to do, and I asked what."

She drew breath. "Yes, well – I'm going to the open-air m-museum, and – and. . . ." It was ridiculous, but she could think of nowhere else. Perhaps, she thought wildly, it was a sufficiently large place for one to remain all day there, in which case there was no need to say more.

"Plenty of time to go there some other day – won't you stay for lunch?" He put his handsome head on one side and studied her face. "Larissa and I will be much more fun, you know."

She had to laugh at that and was borne away in triumph by Larissa to tidy herself. She was led up the carved staircase at the back of the hall, with its two wings leading to the corridor above, and shown into Larissa's room, an apartment of such comfort that Arabella decided that it wasn't comfort but luxury. She sat down on the little satin-covered stool before the dressing table and ordered her mousy hair and did her face, while Larissa lounged on the bed, with a shocking disregard for its splendid brocade coverlet, and talked about everything under the sun. They went down together presently, to join the doctor in the dining room; large enough to seat twenty guests in comfort round its oval table, and hung, as were so many other walls in the house, with family portraits. The doctor saw her looking at them and remarked smilingly: "There are a great many of us, I'm afraid, but the more forbidding of our ancestors we have in this room, for then we need only share their company at meals."

Arabella, sitting between her host and his sister, found

herself enjoying every moment. She was hungry for a start, and the food was delicious and beautifully served, and over and above that, she felt at ease, so that her stammer disappeared completely and she laughed and talked as though they were old friends. And when, after they had had their coffee in the sitting room, she made another effort to leave, and the doctor made it clear that he intended taking her for a short drive through the Veluwe before tea, she found herself agreeing happily to that as well. Larissa declared that she had friends coming to see her, so Arabella, forgetting her despised raincoat, got into the car beside the doctor and was driven away and out of the town, into the woods and heath of the Veluwe, where he pointed out anything which he thought might interest her, and told her titbits of history and tales of the country through which they were passing.

Arabella hadn't enjoyed such a delightful outing for a long time; it seemed to her that she and the doctor had known each other all their lives, and when her wretched stammer returned to lock her tongue rather more tiresomely than usual, and she declared apologetically: "I'm sorry about my stammer; it's only bad when I get excited or upset," he had replied casually: "Don't worry about it, I rather like it."

They were driving through woods now, the trees around them rustling in the wind, shedding their tinted leaves. "I always thought that Holland was flat all over," observed Arabella, "just fields, you know, and cows."

"Well, so it is, a good deal of it, although round Rotterdam there is a vast industrial complex, but here in the Veluwe we have neither – the Dutch come here for their holidays, and some of us are fortunate enough to live here. Perhaps we are a little old-fashioned in our way of life, but on the whole, we are content too." He glanced at her. "You like country life, Arabella?"

"Yes – I'd hate to live in London for ever; I feel lost there."

"So what will you do when you have finished your training? Get married?"

She stared ahead of her at the quiet road unfolding before them. "I should like that," she said soberly, "but chance would be a fine thing." She swallowed the stammer resolutely. "I'm rather a plain girl."

She liked him for not denying the fact, but saying briskly: "Men marry plain girls every day of the week, and nobody is completely plain, you know. When you look in the mirror you see your face completely without expression. Others see differently – besides, men may admire a pretty face, but prettiness isn't another word for happiness, and that's what a man wants in his marriage."

"I'm sure you're right," agreed Arabella politely, "only being pretty does help a girl to get started!"

He laughed then, and after a moment she laughed with him, suddenly not minding being plain at all.

Presently the doctor turned off the road into a country lane running through thick woods, and presently, heathland. "Tea?" he enquired, and without waiting for her to answer: "There's a rather nice place at Leuvenum where you get a pot of tea on a tray and not just a cup without milk, with a biscuit in the saucer."

Which remark led to an interesting talk about food and the customs concerning the eating of it in various countries, which lasted until he drew up before a small-ish hotel in the little town, where, as he had promised her, they were served a tray of tea and offered a selection of cakes which made Arabella's eyes shine with healthy greed. The food at the hospital was good but a little stodgy, she had found; the delicious lunch at the doc-tor's house had served to emphasise that fact. She chose a luscious chocolate and whipped cream confection and ate it with delicate enjoyment, talking all the time, be-cause here at last was someone who seemed to share her thoughts, laugh when she laughed, and be ready to argue without heat when they disagreed. She accepted another cake when her companion pressed her to do so, poured him more tea, and was about to continue some mild argument when her eye caught sight of the clock.

She paused, a forkful of cream and almonds and pastry poised before her open mouth. "The time," she said urgently. "It's almost five o'clock! "

The doctor looked interested. "Are you doing some-thing urgent at that hour?" he wanted to know.

"No – no, of course not, only it's so l-late. I've taken up the whole of your afternoon as well as the morning. I'm sure you must want to get back."

"Why?" he asked, still blandly interested.

Arabella frowned, because he wasn't being at all help-ful. "I d-don't know why you sh-should want to g-get

67

back," she informed him severely. "It's n-none of my business, it's j-just that I don't want you t-to waste your t-time."

"I'm not," he told her simply, so that she gave up, laughing.

"Well, it's been very kind of you to take me round like this, I've enjoyed it enormously," she assured him, "especially in a Bentley."

He smiled idly, lolling back in his chair. "Do you drive?" he wanted to know. "I imagine so, for you knew what to do when the bus crashed."

"However did you know . . .?" she began, quite mystified.

"I asked some of the children. Were you not frightened?"

"Terrified, especially when I saw you coming straight at us." She caught her breath at the memory. "All I could think about was those children, strapped in and unable to help themselves."

His smile was kind. "I believe that you are a brave girl, Arabella."

She flushed faintly. "No, I'm not. I was scared stiff."

"Therefore brave. Shall we go? I thought we might take another road home."

They were at the doctor's house by half past six, and when he invited Arabella to get out of the car, she hesitated, uncertain what to say, for if she stated that she wanted to go back to the hospital, it might sound as if she was tired of his company. On the other hand, if she went indoors with him, he might think she was expecting

68

to be asked to dinner. He solved the vexed question for her.

"Just time for a drink before dinner," he assured her bracingly. "Come along in." And he caught her hand and didn't let it go until they were in the hall once more.

Hours later, lying in bed in her room at the hospital, Arabella went carefully over her day. It had been wonderful; she hadn't been so happy for a long time. Dinner had been a delightful, leisurely meal, with the three of them talking like lifelong friends, and she remembered happily, she hadn't stammered once. She had felt relaxed and at ease, which when she thought about it seemed strange, for she scarcely knew the doctor, and his sister not at all.

She and the children were to go to the doctor's house in two days' time, that he had decided before she had left after dinner. "Before sending you all back to England," he had declared cheerfully, and Arabella, remembering his words very clearly, was conscious of sadness at the idea of leaving the quiet little town and the hospital where everyone was so friendly. Just before she went to sleep she added another thought to the effect that she felt sad at the idea of leaving the doctor too.

CHAPTER FOUR

THE planned move was made, with the wildly excited children, their wheelchairs and possessions, stowed expertly in the Bentley, with Arabella crushed between them, intent on maintaining their balance.

It was late afternoon when they finally got away, with a rousing send-off from those in the hospital who had the time to come to the forecourt and wave goodbye, and because the doctor didn't want the children to feel bewildered as to where they were going, he drove slowly down the main street, while Arabella pointed out the shops she would take them to see if they were good. The worrying thought that she would be unable to push two chairs at once crossed her mind, but as no one else seemed to have noticed this drawback, she forbore from commenting upon it. But she was wrong; someone had noticed. When they arrived at the house and the children were being carried inside, Doctor van der Vorst said carelessly: "There will be someone to go with you when you take the children out – naturally they must go together." He ushered her after the children, saying: "Never mind the luggage, we'll see to that presently."

The children were taken straight to their room and sat in the chairs put ready for them, each with its adjustable table so that they could have their playthings to hand. There were two small hospital beds too, each in a corner, and through the open door Arabella could see the small room which was to be hers. There were flowers everywhere, and a portable T.V. in another corner, and George waiting to greet everyone.

It was a tremendous improvement on the hospital, however kind and thoughtful everyone had been there; here they would settle down to a semblance of home life once again, and by the time they got home once more, their memories of the accident would have faded, and their almost wasted legs be nicely on the mend under the plaster. They were already a good deal more co-ordinated, and their speech had improved enormously; in a week or so they would be fit to travel home.

"Come and see your room," invited Larissa. "Gideon can handle those two for five minutes – they're used to him, aren't they? There's a young girl who comes in to clean each morning, she's very kind and the eldest of several children, we thought she might do to relieve you each day – what do you think?"

"It sounds marvellous," said Arabella a little shyly. Her own family had always been kind to her, but they had never put themselves out for her comfort; but here were people – almost strangers – thinking about her leisure hours before she had even earned any, and a good deal of time and thought must have been spent in preparing the rooms – her own little room had been stripped of its original furniture and was now a charming bedroom, with a little satinwood bed, matched by a bow-legged table with a mirror, a scattering of comfortable chairs and a bedside table upon which reposed a bowl of flowers and a small pile of books.

"Good, then that's settled," said Larissa cheerfully. "Let's get Billy and Sally settled in, shall we? I thought supper and then bed, if that suits you. They'll be all right to leave for a while?"

Arabella was doubtful. "Well, on the ward there was always a nurse – would you mind if I had my supper here?"

"I mind very much." Doctor van der Vorst's hearing must be very sharp, thought Arabella, for he hadn't been anywhere near them. "Hanneke will be glad to come for a couple of hours." He looked at his sister. "Larissa, get someone to go and fetch her, will you?"

A little high-handed, Arabella considered. Supposing Hanneke didn't want to come? And who was this someone who was to drop everything and fetch the poor girl? She said quickly: "There's really no need to upset anyone, really there isn't, I'm p-perfectly able t-to. . . ."

The doctor was arranging Billy in his chair. "Don't argue, dear girl," he advised her equably. "If you will get Sally fixed up, the pair of them can have their suppers – Larissa will help you." He wandered to the door. "I've a couple of calls to make."

He nodded to her, waved to the children and went away, his place taken almost immediately with Emma and the supper tray. Larissa came back too, and, carefully briefed by Arabella, fed Sally while Arabella guided Billy's earnest efforts. It was a messy business, but he was beginning to do better; time and patience were paying their dividends. Arabella hugged him for being a good boy and began the slow business of getting him undressed, watching, as she did so, Larissa's efforts with Sally; she was managing very well, laughing and talking to the child in a manner which quite won Arabella's heart. She turned on the radio someone had thoughtfully placed on one of the tables, and to the sound of the latest pop music and a good deal of merriment, the two children were got ready for bed. They were tired. Arabella tucked them in, kissed them good night, and warned that dinner would be in half an hour, then parted company with Larissa, to retire to her little room, with the door open so that she could keep a watchful eye on Sally and Billy, and make such repairs to her person as she considered necessary and had time for. She had changed her dress, re-done her hair and face, and was experimenting with a new lipstick, when the young girl Hanneke came tiptoeing in. She smiled and shook hands with Arabella and went without a word to sit in one of the comfortable chairs in the children's room. Obviously someone had primed her as to what was expected of her; after a few minutes, satisfied that Hanneke knew what she was about, Arabella crept from the room, in search of Larissa.

In the hall, she hesitated. Larissa had said that dinner would be in half an hour; should she have stopped in her room and waited for someone to fetch her? Or in this large and well-run house, would there be a dinner gong? She hung around for a few minutes and had just decided to go back to her room when the front door opened and the doctor came in.

"Held up, as usual," he remarked without preamble. "Come into the sitting room and I'll give you a drink; Larissa won't be long, though she usually takes ages dressing – always has."

He had put his bag down on one of the wall tables and thrown an arm across her shoulders as he was speaking, and they went together into the sitting room. Once there, and their drinks poured, he was in no hurry to be gone. She suspected that he was putting her at her ease, for he was talking of nothing in particular, and it wasn't until Larissa appeared, looking quite beautiful in a simple little dress which wasn't simple at all when one really looked at it, that he went away to his own room.

"Doctors!" sighed his sister. "If we manage to have a meal at the time I arrange, I am too surprised to eat it. It is always the same," she smiled at Arabella. "Do not marry a doctor." She sipped her drink and added thoughtfully: "Or perhaps you should."

The doctor returned presently, looking as though he had done no work all day; immaculate in his grey cloth suit, his silk shirt and rather dashing tie. He grinned at them as he came in, asked: "Quick, wasn't I?" in a pleased voice and added: "I'm famished."

Dinner was a merry meal. Arabella, who in her own quiet way was a good conversationalist, bloomed under the kindly attentions of her host and his sister; they neither seemed to notice her stammer, and presently she forgot about it too. It was nice to talk freely and to be listened to as though it really mattered what she said. They sat round the dinner table long after they had finished their meal, talking about a great many things, and when finally, after another hour over the coffee cups in the sitting room, she went to bed, Arabella glowed with content and pleasure. She hadn't expected it to be like this; she curled up in her pretty bed after making sure that the children were asleep, and wished with all her heart that she could stay for ever. She liked Doesburg, she liked the house, and she liked the doctor and his sister – especially did she like the doctor. She warned herself not to like him too much just as she was on the edge of sleep.

She was up early the next morning, not earlier than Hanneke, who came in quietly with a cup of tea and indicated that she would stay with the children while Arabella went upstairs and had her bath.

No one, thought Arabella, skipping up the well-polished staircase, had mentioned where the bathroom would be, and surely, in a house of this size, there would be more than one? At the top of the stairs, she stood uncertain. All the doors looked alike; white-painted with swags of fruit and flowers carved above each one. There was a narrow passage at the back of the main corridor. Arabella pattered towards it, for it seemed the most likely place to start looking – besides, presumably the doctor's room was in the front of the house, as Larissa's was, so there would be no fear of her disturbing anyone if she opened the wrong door.

She almost jumped out of her skin when the doctor's voice boomed from behind her: "If it's a bathroom you're looking for, there's one at the end of that passage, or that door over there," he nodded to the other end of the main corridor. "Use whichever one you wish. We shan't disturb you, we each have our own."

She had spun round in a whirl of pink quilted dressing gown, a curtain of pale brown hair and an armful of towels. "Oh, you startled me!" she accused him in a whisper. "I thought everyone was still in bed."

She peered at him through her mousy hair; he was dressed in slacks and a sweater and George was panting happily beside him.

"I get up early," he told her in an answering whisper, and walked towards her, and Arabella, suddenly uncertain and hopelessly behind the times when it came to the correct behaviour towards handsome men she might encounter in her dressing gown, retreated before him.

At the end of the passage, when she could go no further, he reached past her and opened a door. "The bathroom," he pointed out blandly, and stood looking down at her with a kind of surprised amusement. "How old are you, Arabella? – I forget."

"Twenty-two." She shivered a little, although she wasn't cold.

"So old?" he was gently mocking, "but not old in experience, I suspect."

"Well, I've done my t-training as a ch-children's nurse," she assured him earnestly. "I know I've almost another year to do at W-Wickham's, but I understand ch-children, really I do, even though I've n-not had much experience."

She stared up at him, suddenly terrified that he would

76

tell her that she wasn't quite what he wanted for Billy and Sally; that he knew of someone older, better qualified. He said none of these things, however. His: "No, dear girl," was so gentle that she hardly heard it, and when he bent and kissed her cheek, that was gentle too.

She didn't see him until much later in the day. She had got Sally and Billy up, given them their breakfasts with Hanneke's help, and then enjoyed a short break for a cup of coffee with Larissa, while the children, safely strapped in their wheelchairs, sat close to them in the garden, and presently they each took a chair and strolled round the pleasantly winding paths, pointing out things of interest, pausing to examine an abandoned bird's nest, pick an odd flower here and there, and watch a squirrel's antics. The large swimming pool, almost concealed behind a high hedge, was a complete surprise to Arabella.

"Oh, super!" she exclaimed. "You don't suppose the children? . . . no, of course not."

"But of course," said Larissa instantly. "But what about their plasters?"

Arabella frowned in thought, then grinned suddenly. "Plastic pillow-cases, tied round the top. Only I haven't any."

"I can get those. How about swimsuits?"

"I could buy those."

Larissa nodded. "Hanneke will be back in half an hour; you could take them down to the town – that's if you don't mind the walk? Otherwise I'll get my car out."

Arabela was quite shocked. "There's no need, thanks

all the same, for the walk will be good for the children. Do you suppose we could try out the pool this afternoon while the weather's so good?"

Larissa nodded. "Of course. I'll come and help you if you'll let me. Hanneke will go home after lunch and come back after tea to help with bedtime."

"It's all so well planned," commented Arabella wonderingly. "I quite expected to be on my own."

"Good lord, you've got them from dawn to dusk, more or less, and all night too – I'd want a posse of helpers if I were in your shoes." Larissa glanced at her watch. "I must go, but Hanneke will be here very shortly. You're all right alone?"

Arabella assured her that she was; two children, small and light, even if very nearly helpless, were child's play compared to duty on a heavy ward with its quota of drips, injections, dressings, treatments and patients going to X-Ray, Physio, the theatre, not to mention the irritable ones, who needed coaxing into a state of calm, and those in pain, or sleepless. They were unending in their demands on her time and patience – but Billy and Sally, bless them, accepted everything with cheerful faces, and if and when they suffered a small rage over something or other, Arabella accepted them in her turn, her kind heart torn with pity for their plight.

The visit to the shops was a riotous success, with a good deal of giggling on the children's part because Hanneke talked to them in her own language, not worrying in the least that they couldn't understand a word of it and laughing with them when they laughed at her. Ara-

78

bella, praying that someone would understand what she wanted, went into the first likely shop and discovered to her delight that the assistant's English was more than tolerable. She purchased swimwear for the three of them from the small stock available, and they turned for home.

The children's dinner took a long time and because of that, they had it served at noon, so Arabella had time to feed them and settle them down for their nap before her own lunch. They munched their way through their meal, with Arabella sitting between them, helping one and feeding the other. She didn't mind, she had done it before and would doubtless do it hundreds of times more, and when they had at last finished, she saw to their little wants and tucked them into their beds, leaving Hanneke in charge.

The doctor wasn't at lunch. Larissa, sharing the well-cooked, simple meal with her, observed lightly that he had been held up on his morning round. "He quite often is," she explained, "but you know enough about doctors to know that, don't you?" She smiled in a friendly way. "Which reminds me, I have the plastic pillow-cases. When do we go to the pool?"

Arabella speared the last of her mushroom omelette. "Well, they're resting now and Hanneke's there. When I go back I'll start getting them ready – will two o'clock be too soon?" She glanced out of the window. "The sun's very warm and there's almost no wind."

"Two o'clock it is, then."

"I could manage on my own, you know, quite easily,

one at a time – they're as light as feathers."

The other girl smiled and looked for a moment exactly like her brother.

"I wouldn't miss it for the world. I like having you here, you and the children. I lead a useless kind of life at the moment, I suppose, but I'm getting married in a couple of months and there's no point in starting anything – Dirk is in India at the moment, getting a new hospital on its feet – that is the expression, is it not? He's a doctor also. I think that I am mad to marry him when I have had to live all my life with doctors, first Papa and now Gideon, but at least I know what I am in for."

"You'll live in India?" Arabella was interested in this lovely girl's future.

"Lord, no. Dirk has a lecturing post to go to in Utrecht – there's a medical school there – there is a house waiting for us."

"You must be longing for him to come back," said Arabella, unconsciously wistful.

"I am." Larissa glanced at her and away again. "And you? Do you expect to marry?"

"Me? No." Arabella's voice was falsely cheerful; it was hard to sound as though she didn't mind that possibility in the least; there were any number of unmarried women in the world and probably they were perfectly happy. The sooner she got used to the idea the better.

"I think I'll go and start on Billy and Sally, they're so excited they'll not be able to control themselves as well as usual. Once they're in the water, though, they'll be fine."

The bathing party, after a little manoeuvring, got under way; the pool was warm and sheltered, the children, safe in the girls' arms, shrieked with delight as they floated, their plastered legs looking quite ridiculous in their plastic bags, held as high as possible. It was an awkward business, but seeing their happy faces, Arabella considered it well worth the trouble. She was enjoying herself too, her hair piled anyhow on top of her head, wearing the rather drab blue swim suit which had been all the shop had had to offer her, it did nothing for her at all, whereas Larissa in a brightly flowered bikini brought a good deal of colour to the scene. She was consoling herself that there was no one to see anyway, when a sudden upheaval in the water made her look round, fearful that the awkwardness of floating a child with a leg in plaster had been too much for Larissa. It wasn't Larissa, however, it was the doctor, swimming slowly towards them from the deep end. He greeted them all affably, turned on his back and remarked:

"This is a splendid idea, Arabella – why didn't I think of it?"

Arabella wedged Billy up against the side of the pool, aware of an overwhelming pleasure at seeing the doctor, mingled at the same time with regret that she hadn't done something about her hair and had been unable to buy a more attractive swimsuit. She had her mouth open to answer him when there was another upheaval, and George, who had flopped in too, came paddling towards them. The pool's tranquillity was happily scissored up by the cheerful uproar which ensued, with the children screaming delight, George barking and the girls keeping laughing order. The doctor, still on his back with his eyes closed, said nothing; apparently he was taking a nap.

The children, naturally enough, were unwilling to leave the pool; it was only when the doctor suggested a picnic tea on the lawn while the sun was still warm that they were tempted away, wrapped snugly in enormous towels and carried back to the house, where they were dried, dressed and sat in their wheelchairs again by their three companions. Arabella, shovelling Sally smartly into her clothes, was a little astonished to see how completely the doctor was dealing with Billy; allowing him to do the simple tasks he had been so painstakingly taught, and making short work of everything else.

Larissa had thoughtfully provided towelling robes for herself and Arabella. Arabella's was too large and she had bundled it on, the sash pulled ruthlessly tight round her small waist, the sleeves rolled up; her hair, escaped at last and hanging wetly. She had no doubt that she looked a sight, but it was hardly the time to worry about how she looked. Instant glamour was not for her, unlike Larissa, who looked marvellous.

As for the doctor, he hadn't bothered with a robe. His powerful shoulders glistened still with water; he looked strong enough to break up his surroundings with one hand should he have a mind to do so, but she saw with a warm feeling that he was very gentle with Billy as well as quick and competent. The warm feeling spread; he would be kind to anything or anyone smaller or weaker than himself, she was quite certain of that. She smiled for no reason at all and began to comb Sally's hair.

Larissa had gone to dress. She would be back presently, she had promised, and then Arabella could dress too. "I'll be like lightning," she told them as she opened the door and floated away.

"Lightning? that means half an hour at least," declared the doctor. He glanced at Arabella, shapeless in her robe, busily tidying the room.

"I'll stay here," he volunteered, "while you put something else on." He added deliberately, "That thing doesn't suit you at all."

Arabella was conscious of annoyance. "It happens to be two sizes too large," she told him crushingly, "and here's a towel – you'll catch a chill if you don't give yourself a good rub down."

He grinned, caught the towel she handed him and meekly began to do as she suggested.

She was back in ten minutes, rather pink from a quick shower, neatly dressed in one of the cotton uniforms Wickham's had thoughtfully allowed her to take with her because it would be so practical when looking after the children. She had done her hair in a neat little topknot and used only a very little lipstick. She looked very young, much younger than her twenty-two years – like a clean and healthy little girl, her brown face glowing with the exercise, her generous mouth curved happily – because she was happy, completely so.

The doctor gave her a long thoughtful look, but all he said was a cheerful "See you," as he went away to dress.

They gathered presently in a sunny corner of the garden to eat a large and – because of the children – protracted tea. Finally the doctor lay back on the grass and closed his eyes again, and this time Arabella had no doubt that he really was asleep.

"He was up last night," said Larissa softly, "and I'm sure he didn't get any lunch today, for he wouldn't answer when I asked him." She sighed. "I don't know who will look after him when I marry Dirk; Emma is a darling, so is Hanneke, but they have their work to do. He'll have to get married."

"Well, why doesn't he?" asked Arabella in a whisper, as she wiped Sally's sticky hands, and knew as she said it that she didn't relish the idea of him marrying at all.

Larissa shrugged elegant shoulders. "He knows a great many girls, but he never seems serious with any of them."

"Though women are angels, yet wedlock's the devil," quoted the doctor unexpectedly, his eyes still shut.

Arabella turned an indignant face to his supposedly sleeping one, "Well!" she exclaimed indignantly, her bosom heaving with her strong feelings. "What a thing to say – and how can you possibly know, if you're not. . . ." She stopped; perhaps he had been, even though Larissa had said that he was a bachelor.

"No, I'm not," he agreed placidly, "but I get around, you know, and I'm very observant."

His sister laughed, "Don't sound so horribly smug!" She was playing cat's cradle with infinite patience with Sally.

He opened one eye. "I? My dear sister, I merely

quoted the poet Byron."

"You aren't in the least like him, anyway," declared Arabella astringently, picking up, for the hundredth time and with no sign of impatience, the ball Billy was throwing with awkward, jerky movements. He couldn't manage to catch it, of course, but just to throw it was an achievement which she praised gently each time she put it back into his hands.

The doctor's thick brows lifted. "Hardly – I have no romantic dark looks, I'm afraid, and I burst with rude health."

"I meant your character," Arabella pointed out painstakingly, and he opened both eyes. "That is a charming compliment," he told her blandly, "it deserves a reward. I shall take you to Arnhem to shop on Saturday."

The stammer came back with a rush. "H-how k-kind, but I have very l-little money, I'm afraid."

"Ah, I forgot to tell you, someone or other at Wickham's asked me to advance you your salary for the month. Does that make sense to you?"

His eyes were closed again, his face placid. Her salary wasn't due for a week or more, but perhaps the office had thought it would be easier if she were paid while she was in Holland.

"Did they? That would be Mr. Windham from the office, I expect. How thoughtful of him! It will be nice to have some money."

The doctor's closed lids flickered very slightly. "I'll bring it with me when I come home this evening," he promised drowsily.

The money turned out to be a good deal more than she had expected and she said so, to be told that Wickham's had considered that she might need to replace anything lost or damaged during the accident, and she was to regard it as a payment for that purpose; she could sign a form to that effect when she returned. She accepted this explanation without further argument, merely observing that she supposed the hospital was insured against such unfortunate happenings.

"Oh, undoubtedly," replied the doctor. "Do you want to go alone to shop or shall Larissa come with us?"

Arabella hesitated. Perhaps he didn't fancy her company for several hours on end; on the other hand, there was nothing to prevent him from leaving her in a shopping area and collecting her after a reasonable interval. She had few qualms about the language difficulty; there was certain to be someone in one of the larger stores who could speak English, and she had taken the trouble to understand the money. After due thought she said: "Well, I c-could m-manage very well by myself, you know. If you w-would be so k-kind as to set me d-down close to one of the b-bigger shops, then I could meet you again when I'd finished."

The doctor was showing Sally a picture book he had brought with him. "So you could," he agreed mildly.

It was raining on Saturday. Arabella covered the jersey dress with the despised raincoat, stood meekly by while the doctor gave his careful instructions to Hanneke, reminded his sister of her responsibilities, and then ushered Arabella out to the car. It was not yet eleven o'clock, for she had been up early and given the children her full attention so that she might be ready when the doctor wished to leave. She got into the car with the pleasurable feeling of a child going on a treat. Arnhem was a bare twelve miles away. She joined happily in the doctor's small-talk and when they reached Arnhem looked about her with a good deal of interest. It was a pleasant city with fine buildings and plenty of shops; she could hardly wait to begin on the modest list she had drawn up of the things she really needed; dull articles mostly, for her common sense warned her that despite a whole month's pay and extra besides in her purse, it wouldn't be much use going back to Wickham's penniless. Presumably she would have to pay her own fare back, even if they gave it to her later. . . .

She was frowning over her muddled little sums when her companion remarked casually: "You don't need to keep any money back for your fare – we're to see about that for you from this end. Where would you like to go first? Boutiques? A large store?" He cast a look at the nondescript raincoat. "How about a new mac for a start?" He didn't wait for her reply, but swung the car neatly into a space beside a parking meter and before she could think of a suitable reply, had steered her across the pavement to a row of shops on the other side. Into one of these he walked, taking her with him, and fetched up without hesitation in the rainwear department. Here he lifted an imperious finger at a sales lady, murmured briefly, and then went to sit on a heavily upholstered settee in the centre of the vast, carpeted area, leaving

Arabella, still struggling to tell him that she had no intention of buying a raincoat, and horribly impeded by the stammer.

The sales lady was good at her job; kind and efficient, she had removed the offending English garment and was fastening a brilliant coral P.V.C. mackintosh, cut with a decided swagger, and before Arabella realized what she was doing, she planted a pert little cap on Arabella's mousy head and stood back, beaming.

"Pleasant," she assured Arabella. "The fit is good, no? And the colour does well for the complexion, yes?"

Arabella, looking at herself in the mirror, had to admit that this was so. She looked quite different; her intention to buy nothing but toothpaste and undies and a sensible sweater melted away. "I'll take it," she breathed, and remembered the doctor waiting so patiently on his settee.

He was neither on the settee nor was he waiting patiently; he was right behind her, looking over her shoulder at her reflection.

"Very nice," he remarked, "a different Arabella." He glanced at the sales lady. "Now a dress in that colour would suit you very well."

"B-but I don't want a d-dress," Arabella assured him earnestly, if untruthfully.

"Nonsense," he said lightly, "all girls want dresses." He adopted a wheedling tone. "You could look at one or two while you are here."

Which reminded her to say: "I – I never meant you to come, it's such a waste of your time – I could meet you. . . ."

"You said that before," he reminded her kindly, "but I dislike mooning around by myself – besides, it's raining." He gave her a helpless look. "You wouldn't want me to get wet?"

"No, of course not." She was aware that the conversation didn't ring true, but her mind was taken up with the question of how much money she might dare to spend.

"Good." He turned away to the patient sales lady and said something which made her smile and go to a rail of dresses at the other end of the department, to select an armful. She offered them in turn to Arabella to see, and she, wanting them all, was quite unable to decide which she liked best.

"Have I enough money?" she asked the doctor, debating the possibilities of a coral and brown striped wool dress with a flared skirt.

He puckered his brows and closed his eyes, which gave him the appearance of serious thinking. "Plenty," he said at last. "These won't be expensive, I think you'll find – here, supposing you give me your money and I'll pay up as we go."

"I might spend it all."

He shook his head. "I'll take good care of that. I shall put, let me see . . . a hundred gulden on one side – better still, take it and put it in your handbag."

It seemed a sensible arrangement. She bought the dress and a corduroy pinafore dress in a rich chocolate brown and quite carried away, a creamy silk blouse to go with it. It was only while she was waiting for these delights to be parcelled that she remembered the more sensible items on her list. "Have I any money left?" she asked anxiously. "I didn't quite get the prices. . . . I thought it was twenty-nine gulden for the blouse, but it couldn't be as cheap as that. . . ."

"It seems a reasonable price to me," the doctor spoke soothingly, "and you still have – let me see –" he pulled out a handful of notes and coins from his pocket, "well over seventy gulden left."

She sighed with relief. "Oh, good! There are one or two dull things I have to buy, shall I go and get them? Do you want me to meet you at the car?"

"I'll wait here," he told her, "and collect the parcels."

He stowed the packages in the car and when she would have got in, took her by the arm. "Lunch," he suggested. "There's a rather nice place overlooking the Rhine; I can point out the pictorial aspects of our surroundings while we eat."

Which he did, with a gentle humour and a wealth of detail; afterwards she didn't know which she had enjoyed most, the super food, or the doctor's ramblings about their surroundings. And not content with showing her the view from the restaurant, he strongly advised a walk in the Soesbeek Park, with its stately avenue of trees and quiet lakes, and then, having made sure that she didn't wish to make another expedition to the shops, they took a trip along the Rhine to the Westerbouwing tea garden, and had their tea overlooking the river. It was five o'clock by the time they got back to the car, but Arabella, in a happy daze because she was with someone who made no demands on her and hadn't reminded her that she was rather plain and not very interesting, paid no heed to the time. If she didn't go out again for the rest of her stay in Holland, she assured her companion, she wouldn't mind in the very least; her day had been lovely. She thanked him for it with a fervour which brought a faint surprise to his face.

"You don't get much time to go out?" he probed gently.

"Time? Oh, yes – I. . . ." She paused; she could hardly tell him that days out with young men, and certainly not older, elegant men who drove Bentleys, seldom came her way. She said brightly, "Oh, look, it's stopped raining again."

His lips twitched, but he followed her lead and embarked upon a safe conversation concerning the weather in Holland which took them safely back to Doesburg.

Arabella went straight to the children, so that Hanneke and Larissa could be relieved at last, and when later she went to dinner, it was to find that the doctor had gone out. She sat at table with Larissa, telling her about her purchases, conscious that she would have liked him to have been there too to share the reminiscences of the day with all its pleasures. It was then that the unwelcome thought that perhaps the pleasures had been a little tame for him crossed her mind. Probably he had been doing her a kindness, because he was a kind man, and now, relieved of that duty, he had gone off to enjoy himself in a more sophisticated manner. She found herself wondering who he was with.

CHAPTER FIVE

A WEEK went by, and as the weather had turned to rain and wind, bringing with them the first chill of autumn, Arabella had every excuse to wear the new mackintosh, and on occasion, the new dresses as well. As for the children, they were fitted out, to their delight, with all-enveloping capes, so that, well wrapped up, they could be wheeled out each day. They had improved steadily — the effects of the accident were wearing off; their movements were no longer as jerky and unco-ordinated, and although their speech was slow and sometimes very indistinct, their intelligence was as keen as it ever had been. And Arabella, when the three of them were alone, encouraged them to talk — she read to them too, from a book of Hans Andersen's Fairy Tales she had found on one of the bookshelves, and worked away at their exercises. It was a quiet, almost monotonous life, or would have been but for Larissa's gay company, for the two girls saw a good deal of each other even though Larissa had a busy social life of her own as well as doing her share of the children's chores.

Very often there were friends for lunch, but often too, Arabella found herself lunching alone in the dining room with George for company, for the doctor, although he came home at midday when there were guests, seldom put in an appearance otherwise, and if he did, and found her on her own, he almost always excused himself the moment the meal was finished, and although he made conversation while they ate, she had the impression that he was impatient to be gone. She had worried about this at first and then accepted it philosophically, for had not her aunt told her on a number of occasions that men, especially younger men, liked a woman to entertain them with light conversation, especially at meals, and Arabella was aware that she had no light conversation; she was too conscious of the stammer. Probably she bored the doctor stiff.

It was a day or so after she had come to this unhappy conclusion that she was crossing the hall on her way out for an hour, after seeing the children safely on to their beds and the faithful Hanneke in charge, when the sitting room door opened and a girl she hadn't seen before came out. One of Larissa's friends – or perhaps the doctor's. Arabella smiled at her on her way to the door, but before she could reach it, the girl spoke.

"The mouse!" she exclaimed in passable English. "I would have known you anywhere – Gideon was right; he said that you were a mouse to look at and a mouselike companion." She laughed gently and the sound grated on Arabella's affronted ears. "Also that you stammer – that must be a great affliction to you."

Arabella willed herself to speak unhesitatingly and achieved a: "N-no, it's n-not, you see, I'm u-used t-to it."

"Yes? But perhaps you have friends with much patience?"

Arabella studied the girl. She was very pretty, older than herself and expertly made up, with fair hair cut short like a boy's and way-out clothes. Surely not the doctor's cup of tea? But she didn't know that; she knew very little about him – perhaps he liked fashion-plates with unkind tongues. She said quietly, holding back a fast rising temper: "I don't think my f-friends n-notice that I stammer," and even achieved a smile as she opened the door and went out into the drizzle.

At dinner that evening she treated the doctor with such an icy politeness that it was inevitable that he should waylay her as she went to make sure that the children were sleeping before she joined him and his sister for coffee in the sitting room. He had followed her soft-footed and stopped her as she reached the door by laying a hand on her shoulder to turn her round to face him. "What's the matter with you?" he wanted to know. "Don't you feel well?"

She tried to ignore the hand. "Very well, thank you, Doctor."

"Ah – so it's temper, is it? Someone has ruffled your feathers."

Her usually gentle eyes sparkled with anger. "You mean fur, surely? M-mouse fur."

He didn't take his hand away, indeed, its fellow pinned down her other shoulder with a gentle grip which defied the tentative wriggle with which she had tried to free herself. "Do I? I don't know, you tell me."

She answered with a decided snap: "N-no, I w-won't! It'll t-take too long, b-because I s-stammer."

His eyes narrowed. "Someone said that? They called you a mouse, they – jeered, perhaps, at your stammer?"

"You did."

He shook his head. "I would never jeer at you, Arabella. Perhaps I have called you a mouse from time to time, I may even have mentioned your stammer, or passed some remark when it was mentioned in my hearing. No, someone, hearing me, twisted my words into jeers and pity. Is that it?" He gave her a small shake. "Who was it?"

"A very pretty girl with short hair and lovely way-out clothes, who was here this afternoon," mumbled Arabella. "One of your girl-friends, I daresay," she added crossly.

His eyes widened with laughter. "One of them? I am flattered, Arabella. I think I know who you mean, though Elsa van Oppen, who is not, I might add, one of my girl-friends." He grinned suddenly and disarmingly, "Just at the moment I haven't a girl-friend, although I am beginning to think. . . ." He bent his head and kissed her lightly on her mouth, turned her round, opened the door and gave her a gentle push. "Get along with you, Arabella," he said in a voice which might have been an older brother's.

When she went back to the sitting room ten minutes later he had gone out, which was a good thing, for she felt, to her surprise, shy at seeing him again. Despite her homely little face she had been kissed on a number of occasions, but never for the right reasons; because it was Christmas, and the housemen at Wickham's went round

95

kissing everyone from old Sister Blake who was due to retire, to the newest student nurse; by casual friends of the family, overcome by some event which had nothing to do with herself, or by one of Hilary's admirers, carried away by feelings which she herself had never engendered. But the doctor's kiss, casual as it was, had stirred her strangely.

He was sitting alone at breakfast the next morning though, with a pile of letters to read. She wished him good morning, received a cup of coffee from him and took a roll from the bread basket he offered her, an open letter still clutched in his other hand. She put the roll on her plate and sat staring at it, and then, anxious to appear normal, buttered some of it and started her breakfast. What a ridiculous, unlikely place in which to make such a monumental discovery, she was thinking; she had always imagined that people fell in love on moonlight nights, or on a dance floor during the last waltz, even drifting along a river in a canoe – not at the breakfast table at eight o'clock in the morning. For that was what she had done; fallen in love with the doctor. That was why she had been so happy, she supposed. She sipped her coffee and knew that she wasn't going to be quite as happy as that any more. She and the doctor got on very well together, but that was all, at least on his side. She would have to take care.

"Why are you frowning?" asked the doctor suddenly, "Are the children worrying you?"

"No – they're fine, I was just planning our day." She smiled at him across the expanse of white damask between them. "It's tomorrow that they are to be X-rayed, isn't it?"

He had picked up another letter. "Yes – ten o'clock. There will be an ambulance here at half past nine." He began to read, forgetting her at once.

The children regarded the visit to the hospital as an outing; they were boisterous at the very idea of it and consequently jerkier than usual in their movements. But they had no objection to being X-rayed – the whole business went off a great deal better than Arabella had dared to hope. She took them back to the doctor's house in time for their midday dinner, without having set eyes on Doctor van der Vorst. He wasn't at lunch either, and although Larissa was chatty about the children and her own morning, she had nothing to say about her brother. It was absurd, thought Arabella, that she found it quite impossible to mention him, just because she had fallen in love with him. She would have to adopt a more sensible attitude towards the situation if she was to pass the remaining days of their stay in any degree of comfort of mind. She was quite unable to think how she should set about this, for just to think of him sent her heart knocking against her ribs and a pleasant tingle up her spine.

She wrenched her mind away from the fascination of thinking about him and begged her companion to tell her more of her wedding plans – a surefire subject, calculated to keep them both occupied for any length of time.

It was too chilly to take the children out after their afternoon rest. Arabella thought with regret of the fun they had had in the swimming pool; she doubted if it

97

would be warm enough for them to use it again, for the weather had changed with unexpected suddenness, and even if it should change again, and she doubted that, she and the children would be gone. She put the thought from her, and with Sally on one side of her, and Billy on the other, began on a highly coloured jigsaw puzzle, for even if neither of them could manage to put the pieces together, they were both expert at seeing where they should go. In the resulting clamorous directions, which took time and patience to understand, Arabella quite failed to hear the door open and the doctor come in.

She was only aware of him when a large, well-kept hand came down over her shoulder, took the piece she was holding from her, and fitted it in where it should go. "Like life," commented Doctor van der Vorst in his pleasant, lazy voice. "We fuss and fret to get the pattern just so, when all we need is patience until what we are looking for turns up under our hands."

Arabella didn't understand him in the least, but it was a nice safe subject; she was on the point of embarking on a chat about puzzles in general and this one in particular, when he took the wind out of her conversational sails by saying: "The children's X-rays are excellent – couldn't be better. They are fit to travel, I propose to send them home in a couple of days' time."

It was like being knocked on the head; surprise had robbed her of her tongue while thoughts of a completely impractical nature hounded and harried themselves in and out of her head. At length she achieved:

"Oh – how n-nice! I'm s-so glad." She turned

brightly to Billy.

"You hear what the doctor s-says, Billy? We're g-going home in t-two d-days."

Her gaiety sounded hollow to her, but no one else seemed to find anything wrong with it, the doctor made a few remarks relevant to the journey and went away again, leaving her to deal with the excited children. Hanneke had a half day free; Arabella gave Billy and Sally their tea in their room, pleading that the news had made them a little agitated, and then because she didn't care to leave them alone in that state, settled down to read to them. Larissa, who had offered tea before she herself had gone out, had already left the house, and she supposed the doctor to be out too. It was a pity that having refused tea so definitely, she now longed for this refreshment above anything else. True, she had only to ring the bell and ask Emma to bring some, but this was something she couldn't bring herself to do. Emma had been a tower of strength since the children had come to the house, and heaven knew she must have had a great deal of extra work thrust upon her. Arabella drank a glass of water from the tap in the cloakroom and plunged anew into the Tale of the Pie and the Patty Pan. It wasn't one of her favourites, but the children loved it.

"There began to be a pleasant smell of baked mouse," she read, and:

"My dear girl – must you? I have a soft spot for mice, but definitely not baked. Why are you sitting here? Larissa had her tea hours ago, but I have been waiting for you – where is Hanneke?"

Probably no one had told him. She explained patiently about Hanneke going to a cousin's wedding, which, she had been informed, would go on until well into the night.

He nodded understandingly. "They set great store by weddings in this country, you know." He was drawing a face on Billy's plaster, his handsome head close to the small boy's. He didn't look up from this absorbing task when he asked: "And do you set great store by weddings, Arabella?"

She said, "Yes, I do," and then, carried away on a wave of recklessness: "And orange blossom and proposals and f-falling in l-love." She stopped abruptly, aware that she sounded like a fool.

He added a heavy moustache to the face and a pair of outstanding ears. "So do I," he told her placidly as he got up and rang the wall bell by the fireplace, and when Emma had come and he had spoken to her, he asked: "Why, if you did not wish to have tea with us, did you not ring? Emma tells me that it was because Hanneke wasn't here that you remained here — surely you know that you had only to mention this for someone to relieve you for half an hour?"

"Yes, I k-know, but Emma has s-so much to do — she has no t-time to s-spare — I was quite c-comfortable. . . ."

"My dear girl, you don't suppose that this house is run by Emma and Hanneke alone, do you? But perhaps you do, for you see very little of the place other than this room and the sitting room and dining room. There is

100

Juffrouw Blind who comes each day to clean, besides another niece of Emma's who helps her in the kitchen. Either of these ladies would have been perfectly willing to sit with the children."

"Well, I didn't know that, did I?" Arabella answered snappishly, and was instantly contrite at his warm:

"No – how could you? I should have thought of such things, especially when Larissa is out." He turned to speak to Emma, still waiting beside him. "Emma will take tea into the sitting room and Juffrouw Blind will sit with the children."

So Arabella had her tea, and fingers of hot buttered toast with it, not to mention tiny, paper-thin biscuits and a rich fruit cake, the latter especially for the doctor's benefit because he had a strong partiality for it. They talked comfortable nothings and not a word was said about the journey. Afterwards Arabella wondered uneasily if she had talked too much about herself. The doctor hadn't seemed to ask questions, but she had found herself telling him about her parents and her life with her aunt and uncle, but not, if her memory served her faithfully, very much about Hilary, for she had been conscious of a strong desire – quite hopeless, she realized – to keep the doctor to herself, and once Hilary had found out about him she was quite capable of finding a way to meet him. And at dinner that evening, very aware of his large, amiable presence at the head of the table, her determination to keep these few weeks in his house as a secret memory became even stronger. She had mentioned him in her letters home, but she had never described him, she hoped now that her family, and especially Hilary, would imagine him to be dull and middle-aged.

She speared a forkful of Emma's delicious Peach Melba and then let it fall again at the doctor's soft enquiry: "Deep thinking, Arabella? What about, or should I not ask?"

She said almost guiltily: "Nothing ... that is ..." she searched feverishly for some lighthearted reply and achieved only another, "nothing."

He was far too nice to tease her; he began to talk of something else immediately, and she loved him, if that were possible, a little more for his tactful kindness.

It wasn't until late the following evening that she saw him again, for he had been from home all day. She had had her bath, brushed her hair and hopefully applied a cream to her face which guaranteed to keep it youthful for ever; now she was pottering silently about the children's room, getting out clean clothes for the morning. When there was a light tap on the door, she called a soft "come in", supposing it to be Larissa.

It wasn't Larissa but the doctor, who glanced at her briefly. "Hullo – sorry to bother you at so late an hour. Can you be ready to leave after lunch tomorrow?"

She stood by the pillow cupboard, quite dwarfed by its carved magnificence, her arms full of small garments. Her heart, surprised at the sight of him, had tripped and raced on happily; now it hung like a leaden thing in her chest. She said with care, because she didn't want to stammer: "Yes, of course. I can pack in a very short time and be ready to leave when you wish – we haven't much with us. Are the children to know?"

He didn't answer her at once, but stood leaning against the wall, his hands in his pockets. "Not caught unawares, Arabella?" he asked. And when she didn't answer him: "I think the children might be told after breakfast, don't you? See that they have a simple lunch – they'll travel better that way. They should be home for their supper."

"Home?"

"Wickham's. They will have a check-up there and go home the next day. It will be a long journey for them."

A very long journey, she thought sadly, taking me away from you for the rest of my life.

He strolled nearer, to stand before her studying her intently.

"You have beautiful hair," he said at length. And indeed, in the subdued light from the one lamp she had switched on, its mousiness had taken on a pleasant soft brown and there was no denying its length.

"What's that on your face?" he wanted to know.

"A nourishing cream," she explained seriously. "It's to k-keep me y-young."

He gave a whispered bellow of laughter. "But you are young, dear girl." He paused. "Do you know how old I am?"

She shook her head. "No." She smiled suddenly and a dimple showed briefly in one faintly pink cheek. "Would you like to borrow some of my cream?"

She hadn't noticed him move, but now he was as close

as he could get.

"Impertinent girl," he said, and wrapped her in a vicelike grip to kiss her. "I'm thirty-eight," he told her in a perfectly ordinary voice; evidently the kiss had had no effect upon him at all. "Do you find that old, Arabella?"

But the kiss had had an effect upon her; she had no breath to speak of, certainly not to waste on speech. She shook her head and hoped that he couldn't hear her heart thundering under her dressing gown.

He stared down at her for a long moment. "Good," he said softly, and smiled as he bent to kiss her once more, only this time it was a gentle kiss. His good night was gentle too. She still hadn't said a word when he went out of the room.

She spent a miserable night, alternating between delightful memories and the bleak knowledge that she would be going away in a few hours and would never see the doctor again. She wondered if, supposing she could have stayed a little longer, he might have fallen in love with her. He was a little interested, but only, common sense told her, a little. She got out of bed and switched on the light over the dressing table to peer at herself in the triple mirror. Her anxious eyes stared back from a tired face; she was forced to admit that, with all the optimism in the world, she had no looks to speak of. Her aunt had been quite right when she had told her with her habitual vague kindliness years ago, that she would never be a pretty girl. "Although you have a pleasant manner," she had said, "and good health."

Just for a time, thought Arabella rebelliously, examining her unremarkable profile, it would be delightful to exchange both her pleasant manner and her undoubted good health for a unpleasant disposition and shattering good looks. She got back into bed presently, and because she had plenty of good sense and she had a long day before her, she went to sleep.

She was taken aback to discover that Sally and Billy didn't want to go home after all. They loved George, they told her, agitation making their speech worse than usual, and they loved Crosby and Tatters and the kittens and everyone else in the house – and would they never see the doctor again, or Arabella?

She provided suitable soothing answers to these questions, painted a reassuring picture of home, and packed their things before wheeling them, with Larissa to help, round the rambling old house to say goodbye to everyone. She said her own goodbyes at the same time, although Larissa and Hanneke insisted on helping her with the children's lunch, a meal they neither wanted nor ate much of. They were swallowing the last reluctant mouthfuls when the doctor joined them, wanting to know cheerfully who was ready to go home. Two glowering small faces stared up at him as Arabella made haste to assure him that once they were on the way, everything would be all right. And presently she left Hanneke in charge and went to have her own lunch in the company of the doctor and his sister. She made as sorry a meal as the children had done, pushing the food round and round her plate and keeping up an overbright conversation about nothing at all. She was eager to be gone now; there was no sense in dragging out a situation which had become as painful as she could bear. When coffee came at last she drank hers quickly.

"If you will excuse me," she spoke to Larissa, "I'll go and put the finishing touches to the children – I daresay the ambulance will be here at any moment."

"No, it won't," said the doctor calmly, and passed his cup to have it refilled. "You're coming with me."

"With you?" breathed Arabella, not understanding in the least.

"That's right. I told you you would be going home on the same route as you came, only this time I'm taking it." He glanced at her briefly. "I go to England fairly frequently; it just so happens that I have some business there and it's convenient for me to go today. Do you suppose you can manage on the journey?"

Arabella remembered managing twenty-two children on the way over, with Sister Brewster sitting at the back, issuing orders and doing nothing to help. "Easily," she told him, and smiled. The day had suddenly become perfect; it stretched before her, hours and hours of it in the doctor's company, all the way to Wickham's.

"How like Gideon," remarked Larissa laughingly, "not to tell you. How I shall miss you, Arabella, and how dull it is going to be until I get married. Thank heaven there isn't much longer to wait for the wedding. You couldn't come over for it, I suppose?"

"Well, n-no, I d-don't think so. You see, my holidays have had t-to be changed because I had to c-come with

106

the children. I expect I'll have t-to t-take what's left."

Arabella didn't look at the doctor; if he asked her to come to Larissa's wedding, then she would somehow, even if it meant giving in her notice. But nothing so drastic was demanded of her; he remained silent, and after a few more minutes' talk on the girl's part, he suggested that they might make a move.

It took a little time to stow the children, their folding chairs and their odds and ends of luggage in the Bentley. This time they were in the back on their own, propped up with cushions, their wasted little legs planted firmly on some hassocks Larissa had unearthed from the attics. They had cheered up by now, excited at the idea of the long ride in a car, and buoyed up by Larissa's promise to come and see them one day. Arabella tucked the rugs cosily around them and got in beside the doctor. It was raining and decidedly chilly, but she hadn't noticed; she had on the new mackintosh and the perky little cap; the cheerful colour washed her pale face with coral and gave her a false gaiety. She felt secure in it, like a knight behind his armour.

They started off, a cheerful little party despite the last-minute tearful goodbyes, the children's spirits lightened by the bestowing of last-minute gifts by the members of the doctor's household. Arabella turned for a last look as the car stopped at the gates. They were all there, Larissa and Emma, Hanneke and Juffrouw Blind and the niece who worked in the kitchen, as well as the elderly gardener whom she had never got to know. George was there too, being restrained from following them, and she had no doubt that somewhere behind the sitting room windows, Crosby and Tatters and the kittens were watching too. It was like leaving a loved home; she swallowed back strong feelings and said in a little voice: "You must be so glad when you come home again."

He had understood her. "Indeed yes. It holds everything I hold dear – I cannot imagine living anywhere else. I'm glad that you feel like that about it, too."

She stifled regret as they left Doesburg behind and joined the motorway which would carry them on the first stage of their journey to Calais. Regret was a waste of time; she only had a few more hours of the doctor's company, and she wasn't going to spoil them.

The journey proved all she could have hoped for; the doctor was at his most amusing, the children were as good as gold, and when they stopped for a picnic tea, they managed very well, draped in plastic bibs and towels, with the doctor attending to Billy's wants, and Arabella seeing to Sally. The children settled, they had a quick cup of tea themselves before pressing on, although the Bentley was making so light of the journey that they had time to spare at Calais and spent it playing with the children until they could board the Hovercraft.

Arabella had been nervous of seasickness during the journey, but Billy and Sally had gone on playing the childish game with no signs of queasiness. Indeed, they hardly noticed their transition to land again, but once on the road again they dozed off, leaving Arabella free to look around her.

"Nice to be back in England?" the doctor wanted to

know. "I expect you're glad. Presumably you will have days off before you go back to your duty on the ward."

"I hadn't thought about it. It would be nice, though. I've th-three weeks' holiday d-due, too."

"Hardly the time of year for holidays, surely?"

"Well, no, b-but I had to postpone them – I was going to Scotland. . . ." She had been on the point of telling him how she had come to be on the ill-fated trip, but that would bring Hilary into it. Instead she said:

"I'll get my uncle to lend me his car and go down to Cornwall – it's lovely in the autumn."

"On your own?" He was tearing up the road to London, keeping to a steady seventy.

"Yes. There won't be anyone else – they will have had their holidays."

"When do you finish your training?" His question started them off on generalities once more.

They reached Wickham's a few minutes after seven o'clock. It looked grey and lifeless although she was well aware that behind those blank windows the place was teeming with life; it didn't seem possible that she had had lunch in Holland, sitting in the doctor's dining room. She closed her eyes in a childish wish to be transported back there once more and opened them to find that the car had drawn up outside the Accident Room entrance and that without any visible effort, the doctor had been surrounded by porters, nurses and the Casualty Officer on duty, who between them unpacked the children and bore them, half asleep, to the children's ward where bed and supper awaited them. That left Arabella, her arms full of the jetsam of the journey, standing in the wide passage leading to the accident room, wondering what she should do first.

The doctor decided that for her. "Matron, I think, don't you? I'll come with you, if I may, and hand Billy and Sally over formally – you too."

"Me?"

"Well, yes, you have been in my care while you were in Holland, have you not?"

"Oh – I hadn't thought of it like that."

They were walking slowly in the direction of the main corridor. He stopped. "How did you think of it?"

She stared up at him. "I – I don't know. I was happy."

She began to walk on again, wishing she hadn't said that. They reached the main corridor and started to cross the back of the vast entrance hall, the main staircase looming beside them. The doctor stopped again. "I was happy too, dear girl," he said quietly, and smiled slowly. The smile warmed her through and through, just for a moment she glowed with happiness, then there was a faint sound on the staircase and the doctor looked over her shoulder and she saw his eyes widen.

"And who, I wonder, is the descending angel?" he wanted to know.

Arabella knew. Even as she turned her head, her foreboding became reality. It was Hilary, looking like every man's dream of the perfect girl.

CHAPTER SIX

THE doctor was right. Hilary looked, even in her Sister's uniform and at the end of a day's work, exactly like a story-book angel, all pink and gold and blue eyes; she looked fragile too, Arabella noted sourly, knowing that under that soft yielding front was a Hilary of steel who always got what she wanted, and did it with such charm that no one realized that they were being ruthlessly conned.

Arabella perceived that she was going to be conned now, she and Doctor van der Vorst. She knew sadly that it would be easy for Hilary to wrap him round her thumb, for she had seen the initial impact of her cousin's appearance upon him, but there was nothing she could do about it, not at the moment. She went to greet her cousin and was caught in a laughing hug and a joyous, "Arabella – how lovely! Miss Trenchard said you would be back today – how lucky that I should come off duty at the very moment. . . ." Hilary's eyes were on the doctor as she spoke and she went on gaily: "This must be Doctor van der Vorst – now why did I imagine you to be middle-aged and dull? for that's the impression Arabella gave us in her letters."

Clever girl, thought Arabella, unwillingly admiring, and watched as Hilary put out a hand before she could get her unwilling tongue to frame an introduction. "I'm

Hilary, Arabella's cousin, you know." She tilted her golden head. "Or perhaps you didn't know?"

Her hand was gently engulfed. "How do you do?" said the doctor formally. "And yes, Arabella has spoken of you. I'm delighted to meet you."

And to Arabella, listening with the unhappy edginess of those in love, he sounded as delighted as he had said he was. I bet you are, she thought vulgarly, watching his slow smile with a pain which was almost physical.

Hilary was wasting no time; she turned briskly to Arabella. "You'd better go straight to Miss Trenchard, ducky," she counselled. "She's on duty this evening – we'll wait here for you, if you like." She shot a glance at the doctor who was staring at her rather hard. "I want to hear all about your stay in Holland. If I'd known I was going to be rescued by you, Doctor van der Vorst, I would have begged Matron on my knees to let me off that stupid Admin. course that prevented me going at the last minute."

"I'm flattered, but it was hardly a social occasion." And when she pouted prettily: "It would have been a delightful surprise to have found you in the wreckage, though."

Arabella had heard enough; she had heard it all before – Hilary getting to work on the man she had singled out for attention – only this time it hurt. It was a pity that, having witnessed so many of these charming little scenes, she had never learned a thing from them to help herself. "I'll go and see Miss Trenchard," she mumbled, and found the doctor beside her.

112

"Yes," he agreed placidly, "I think we should do that," and added apparently for Hilary's benefit: "I feel sure we shall meet again."

It was only the length of the corridor to Miss Trenchard's office, so there was no need to talk. They went in together and the doctor kept her firmly beside him while he and the Matron held a brisk conversation about the whole episode of the accident and its aftermath.

"Nurse Birch was of the greatest possible help," he declared. "She showed great courage and good sense, and took the greatest possible care of the children. I believe that Sally and Billy have improved enormously, for she has been with them constantly. I am afraid that she has lost a good deal of her off duty and she had virtually no days off. Perhaps something could be arranged?"

He spoke in his usual placid tones, but somehow it was obvious that he expected Miss Trenchard to do something about it at once. And she, poor lady, with Arabella's name down to go to Male Surgical at half past seven in the morning, found herself suggesting that Arabella might like to have four days off immediately. The doctor agreed immediately to this without giving Arabella a chance to speak for herself; complimented Miss Trenchard upon the high quality of her nursing staff, so that her somewhat austere face became wreathed in smiles, bade her a courteous goodbye and took his leave of her, taking Arabella, still speechless, with him.

In the corridor she said a little helplessly: "Look, that was awfully kind of you, getting me days off, but there are all sorts of things – I mean I don't even know

113

when to come back on duty – I. . . ."

"Telephone tomorrow. Do you want to pack or anything, or shall we go now?"

"Go where?" asked Arabella, regrettably dim.

"To your home, of course. You didn't imagine that I would leave you high and dry here?"

"Well, yes, I did. I mean, you brought me back, which was awfully kind of you, but you don't need to do any more." She smiled at him, delighted with herself because she hadn't stammered for quite a while. And she had forgotten Hilary.

Which was a mistake; Hilary was waiting for them, just where they had left her. She smiled with charm at both of them, but addressed Arabella, "Well - days off?"

"Yes," said Arabella, hating herself for speaking with reluctance. "Four."

Hilary's blue eyes became intent. "Going home this evening, Bella?"

"Yes," said Arabella unwillingly, and because she knew that Hilary was going to ask: "Doctor van der Vorst is driving me."

Hilary turned a smile of pure enchantment on to the doctor. "Oh, would I be an awful nuisance if I came too? I've a couple of days, but I was going by train in the morning, but it's such a wretched journey. I can be ready in ten minutes." She waited for his reply, contriving to look forlorn.

"I shall be delighted," said the doctor. "I was just asking Arabella if she needed to pack anything." He glanced at Arabella. "Will ten minutes suit you?"

Arabella nodded. She knew exactly what was going to happen; she would sit in the back of the car and Hilary would sit beside him and turn on the full power of her charm. She started along the corridor which led to the Nurses' Home, not waiting for her cousin.

In her room she pushed a few clothes into a case and went to see if any of her friends were about. Anne Morgan was in her room, doing her laundry and making up a clean cap. This she cast carelessly down when she saw Arabella. "We heard that you were coming back, but no one knew when," she exclaimed happily. "What's to do?"

"Days off," said Arabella. "I'm going now."

"How?"

"Doctor van der Vorst is driving me home – he brought us back."

Anne made a face. "Is he awful?" she asked, "or have you got yourself a boy-friend?"

"He's not awful, he's not my boy-friend either. Hilary's coming with us – she's got days off too."

Anne looked up in astonishment. "She has not – whoever told you that? I was behind her in the queue in the canteen, and I heard her telling Sister Fleming that she hadn't any days off due until next week."

Arabella considered this statement. "I expect she fixed them," she gave it her opinion, "because I'm back."

Anne picked up the cap again without looking at her. "Probably. Is this doctor nice-looking?" she asked carelessly.

"Very." Arabella, carried away on a flood of memories, went on: "He's got a gorgeous house, very old and full of lovely things, and he must have a lot of money, because he drives a Bentley. His sister has a car too — there's a swimming pool. . . ." She stared at the wall in front of her, her thoughts so deeply in Holland that she had forgotten where she was.

Anne eyed her closely. "Just right for Hilary," she observed dryly.

Arabella came back to the present with a crash. "Y-yes, that's w-what I th-thought," she agreed, her stammer worse than ever.

The doctor was standing exactly where they had left him, only this time he was talking to Sir Justin Gold, one of the senior consultants at Wickham's. Sir Justin had a big, booming voice and a magnificent bedside manner, but apart from these two things he was a nice man, happily married and a doting father. Arabella liked him, although their acquaintance was of necessity confined to running the great man's errands when he was on the ward. But he always thanked her politely, and once, when she had fallen down with a loaded instrument tray, right at his very feet, he had picked her up and re-arranged the tray for her in a meticulous fashion, which had been a great waste of time, for she had had to go away and re-sterilize the whole lot, but the action had been kindly meant and she hadn't forgotten it. She hung back now, looking, if she did but know it, rather forlorn in her bright mackintosh. She was making up her mind whether to slip away and return in five minutes or so, looking as though she hadn't already been there once, or advance upon the two gentlemen, when the doctor looked up and called:

"Hullo, Arabella – I was just telling Sir Justin about your good work in Doesburg."

She went towards them then, a little reluctantly, and Doctor van der Vorst put out a long arm and caught her gently by the sleeve, pulling her close to him.

"Well, well," observed Sir Justin, "I'm delighted to hear such good things of you, Nurse. A very sensible girl I have always thought you – I'm sure you acquitted yourself with flying colours." He shook his head. "A very unfortunate business; I was sorry to hear about the coach driver – poor fellow." He smiled at Arabella. "I hear that you are to have a few days' well-earned holiday before returning to the wards. I'm sure you deserve them, my dear."

He patted her arm, shook hands with the doctor and made his measured way towards the Surgical side.

"He's nice," observed Arabella without much originality.

"Very – he was one of my examiners."

She twisted round to see his face. "No? Did you know he was here?"

The doctor smiled slowly. "Lord, yes. I pop in and out quite often – medicine's a very international job these days, you know. I've been to see Billy and Sally, by the way."

"So have I. They're happy now they're back." She was about to embark on the plans she had made to see

117

them from time to time when they came to Wickham's for treatment, but she was cut ruthlessly short by her companion's: "Where's Hilary?"

Hilary already, and so eager. She scotched the telling of the plans. "She's coming – I can hear her on the stairs."

They both turned round to look as Hilary tripped towards them. She had a new coat; it was the first thing Arabella noticed, bordered with fur and with a fur-lined hood. It was perhaps a little early in the year for a winter coat, but this one was so eye-catching any girl would be forgiven for wearing it at the first opportunity. She gave the doctor her case to carry and tucked a confiding hand under his arm. "You are a dear," she said with just the right amount of gratitude in her voice. "Poor old Bella must be worn out."

"N-no, I'm n-not," said Arabella sharply, "it w-was a v-very c-comfortable trip." She would have liked to have said a great deal more, but the wretched stammer was back again and she had seen Hilary's tolerant, faintly pitying glance. The three of them went out to the car, and Hilary, just as Arabella had foreseen, urged her to take the back seat so that she could have a nice snooze on the way home. "Don't worry about Doctor van der Vorst," she begged her nettled cousin. "I'll direct him – besides, there's such a lot I want to hear about the accident. You just have forty winks, darling."

Arabella had no wish to take forty winks. She sat in the leather luxury of the Bentley, with her eyes wide open, listening to Hilary's voice, unable to hear what she

118

was saying, but able to hear her light laugh — and the doctor's; he sounded as though he was enjoying himself. She answered politely when one or other of them spoke to her, and tried desperately to think of a way in which she could captivate the doctor's attention. She could think of nothing short of plastic surgery and a wig; she was in quite a nasty temper by the time they reached Braintree, and when the doctor drew up outside the White Hart with the obvious intention of stopping for dinner, and since she had no intention of playing gooseberry, she closed her eyes with commendable speed and when Hilary turned round to speak to her, gave no answer.

"She's asleep," said Hilary, and Arabella could have sworn that she heard satisfaction in her cousin's voice. "Don't let's disturb her, she's tired out. Mother will give her supper in bed when we get home."

She heard the doctor's seat creak as he turned to look at her. "She may be hungry as well as tired," he offered placidly.

"Oh, Gideon —" Gideon already! — "you know how awful it feels to be wakened and made to eat. Leave her."

"She may wake up — I'll leave a note so that she will know where to find us."

Arabella heard the seat creak again and peeped cautiously. The doctor's magnificent head was bent over a pocket book and he was writing; Hilary was watching him, looking faintly put out. They got out of the car then and the doctor opened the back door and laid the note on Arabella's knee. He was so close that his coat sleeve

119

brushed her cheek.

She gave them a minute in which to enter the hotel and then put on the car light and read his note. It said astonishingly: "You look very sweet when you're asleep, even when you're only pretending. Please join us for dinner." It was signed Gideon.

She read it several times. How could he have guessed that she wasn't really asleep? She thought she had been doing it rather well – Hilary had been taken in – or had she? Arabella said pettishly and out loud:

"Well, I won't! I don't want any dinner."

They were away a long time, and long before then she was famished. She sat and stared at the hotel's cheerful lights and thought of all the lovely food beyond its walls. She was still staring when the doctor came out with a tray in his hand, opened the door and arranged it on her knee. "You're an obstinate girl," he greeted her with brisk cheerfulness. "Here's some food, and drink this first."

Sandwiches, she saw with satisfaction, an appetizing pile, and they all looked different. She obediently drank from the glass the doctor was holding out to her and after the first swallow, exclaimed: "Why, it's champagne!"

"Naturally – one should always drink it when one has something to celebrate."

He meant meeting Hilary, of course. She took another sip, bit into a sandwich and said with her mouth full: "Thank you very much, it was kind of you to remember me. . . ."

120

"I don't need to remember," he observed quietly. "Move over, I'm coming in."

She did as she was told, her precious glass held carefully in one hand. "Where's Hilary?" she asked then.

"Putting on a new face, I imagine. There's something I want you to do for me, Arabella."

She took another sip to give her spirits the boost they would most surely need. "Yes?" she asked cautiously.

"Mr. Burns," he began, to surprise her. "I thought I would go and see his wife while I am over here, she might like to know. . . ." He hesitated. "It is sometimes easier to accept something when one is told it rather than be forced to read it or have it telephoned. I imagine Mrs. Burns might find it easier to accept if someone talked to her about her husband's death. I wondered if you would come with me. You were there – you saw it all happen, perhaps you could remember something he said or did – something pleasant. Do you know what I mean?"

"Yes, I do. Of course I'll come. When do you intend going to see her?"

He produced a bottle from somewhere or other and refilled her glass.

"You have four days' holiday, have you not? What about the day after those – in the evening? You come off duty at eight o'clock, I expect. I'll come for you at half past, if you won't be too tired."

"I'll be there," Arabella told him.

He patted her shoulder. "Good girl! Now eat up those sandwiches." He eased himself back on the seat beside her. "Why did you pretend to be asleep, Arabella?"

She choked on her sandwich. "Well, I – I w-was tired."

"As good an excuse as any, I suppose."

"How did you know?"

He smiled at her. "You forget that during the past weeks I have had plenty of opportunities of studying your face."

She had no answer to that, but asked instead: "Did you have a good dinner?"

"Excellent, and very entertaining."

Arabella put the picture of Hilary out of her mind and went on doggedly: "Are you going back to London this evening?"

He turned his head and looked at her. His face was serious, yet she could have sworn that he was laughing behind it. His voice was bland.

"Hilary has kindly invited me to stay the night at your aunt's house."

The delicious smoked salmon sandwich she was eating tasted of dust and ashes. She had to say something, and why hadn't she thought of it? Hilary had. "Oh, yes, of course, there's heaps of r-room. You've been s-so kind, you must be t-tired – my aunt. . . ."

"Don't babble, Arabella," he begged her gently. "Here is Hilary at last. I shall expect something really ravishing after all this while."

He got out to join her cousin and presently helped her into the car, got in beside her and drove on, leaving Arabella to answer her cousin's concerned enquiries as to her tiredness, brush the last of the crumbs carefully away, and ruminate on the strange fact that when she was with the doctor she almost never stammered.

It was a short journey from Braintree. They were welcomed by a surprised and pleased Aunt Maud, and even her uncle welcomed Arabella with unusual warmth. Arabella basked for a few happy moments in their affection before being brought down to earth again.

"Dear child, where did you buy that mackintosh? The colour is far too conspicuous for you – it makes your face quite colourless." Her aunt sounded put out.

"She's tired," said Hilary instantly. "Mother, she must go straight to bed, she's had a long journey – she can tell us her adventures in the morning." She turned to the doctor. "Come into the sitting room, Gideon, and Father will give you a drink." Over her shoulder she flung: "Good night, Bella, sleep well."

Doctor van der Vorst paused. "Good night, Arabella," he spoke quietly. "I shall see you in the morning."

Arabella wanted to stay very badly, but she had been dismissed – quite kindly, but dismissed all the same. Her aunt was already fussing round her with offers of a hot bath and warm milk; she couldn't remember her ever having done that before. Perhaps, she thought shrewdly, it was to impress the doctor. She gave him a cold look. "Oh, I expect so," her good night was cold too.

She trailed upstairs after her aunt, who only stayed for two minutes after all, excusing herself on the plea

123

that she had to make sure a guest room was ready for the doctor and telling Arabella, quite nicely, that she could fetch her milk from the kitchen.

So Arabella, by now in a towering rage, had her bath and then crept down the back stairs to the kitchen, where she ate several slices of bread and butter, drank two glasses of cooking sherry she found in one of the cupboards, and then sat on the table eating a couple of bananas and a wedge of the Stilton cheese specially kept for her uncle's consumption. She felt better after that, although the sherry had tasted rather awful. She went back to her room and then out of its door again to hang over the banisters and listen to the murmur of voices coming from the drawing room. A good cry would have helped, but she was past crying by now. She trailed back to her room and got into bed, where she stayed awake until she heard everyone come up to bed. The last thing she heard was Hilary's tinkle of laughter.

She was down early for breakfast after a quick visit to Nanny, who was sitting up in bed, drinking her morning tea. She nodded in answer to Arabella's bald statement that she had come back, and said, mumbling a little because she hadn't got her teeth in: "I can see you need someone to talk to, child. Come and have tea with me this afternoon, all cosy in the nursery. You won't be missed." Her voice was dry.

The twins followed Arabella downstairs and then her aunt, who greeted her kindly, hoped that she had slept well, expressed an insincere wish to hear all about Arabella's adventures as soon as she had an hour to spare,

124

and begged her to go with the twins to the rectory where the Rector's wife had promised to leave a quantity of apples ready to be collected. "Too many for the twins," said their mother positively, "so I thought you might like to go along with them – the walk, you know, and all that lovely fresh air."

Arabella bit back several arguments in favour of not going. There was no sign of the doctor, indeed, it was still not yet eight o'clock; there would be plenty of time to see him before he went, and it really didn't matter any more. He had gone, so to speak, already, from the moment he had cast his eyes upon Hilary. She finished her breakfast, pulled on an old coat which had served her for errands for countless years, and set off with the twins.

The Rectory wasn't far – ten minutes' walk; but the twins didn't like walking straight to somewhere and back again, so there was a good deal of deviation from the road so that they might examine the mole-hills in one of the fields, watch a water rat or two, and stand patiently under a tree in the hope of seeing a squirrel. Arabella goodnaturedly went with them; it was quite half an hour later by the time they reached the Rectory.

There were several baskets of apples, and Arabella wondered why her aunt hadn't suggested that she should have taken the car in order to fetch them. The three of them set off for home, laden with baskets, the twins munching and quarrelling mildly while Arabella thought about Bertie Palmer, the Rector's son, home on holiday. She disliked him – he was a weedy young man with a

125

great sense of importance, and what was worse, he always knew better than anyone else, which made conversation difficult and sometimes wellnigh impossible. She dismissed him from her thoughts and concentrated upon the doctor, which wasn't in the least difficult, and she was still thinking about him when they reached Little Dean House.

Hilary was on the lawn at the side of the house and Doctor van der Vorst was with her. Even from that distance Arabella could see that Hilary had a hand tucked under his arm and he was laughing down at her as though there were no one else in the world. Arabella, feeling sick, said: "Leave the apples there, I'll take mine round to the kitchen and get someone to fetch them presently. You'd better go and say good morning to Doctor van der Vorst."

They went off obediently and she rounded the corner of the house, opened the kitchen door, dumped the apples on the table, poured herself some coffee from the pot on the stove and sat down in the old rocking chair by the Aga. She didn't bother to look up when the door opened; for she supposed it to be Mary the cook, but she paused in her sipping to say: "There are the apples on the table, there are heaps more outside – someone can bring them in presently."

"Good morning, Arabella," said the doctor, and set the rest of the fruit down on the table. "You were out early. You had friends – a friend perhaps, to visit? Hilary tells me that you and the Rector's son were practically brought up together."

She stared at him. "B-Bertie?" she asked, her eyes round. "Well, we had lessons together – why on earth ..." She remembered very vividly how, as a five-year-old and a not very happy one at that, she had detested Bertie.

The doctor went on blandly: "You saw him this morning?"

"Well, of course – he's on holiday, you know." She got up and went over to the table and took an apple and bit into it, then remembering her manners, offered one to her companion, who followed suit.

"He's – he's ..." she began, longing to tell the doctor in a few crisp sentences just how awful Bertie was, but was interrupted by Hilary's entrance.

"Darling," began her cousin, "there you are – what a chore for you going over to the Rectory with the twins, but I suppose it was as good an excuse as any ... did you see Bertie?"

"Of course I saw him," said Arabella, nettled at all the questions. All this fuss about a young man she heartily detested! "Why?"

Hilary threw her a laughing glance. "Never mind, love. Mother wants you to find that knitting pattern she says she lent you, you know the one, that *Vogue* waistcoat with the pattern that took you a week to work out."

"Now?" Arabella looked at the doctor, who wasn't looking at her, but at Hilary. There was no point in her staying, so she walked to the door, pausing only to ask: "When are you going, Doctor? Shall I see you before you leave?"

"Your aunt has kindly asked me to stay another night – I'll take Hilary back tomorrow evening. Too soon for you, I suppose?" He gave her an intent look which she found disconcerting. "You will want to stay until the last minute."

"Yes, thank you all the same."

It took Arabella half an hour to find the pattern and long before then she had seen the Bentley going down the drive with Hilary beside the doctor. They weren't back for lunch, and Arabella, for once ignoring her aunt's request to escort the twins to neighbouring friends for an afternoon's games and tea, dragged on her old coat and went for a walk through the woods and along the lane to Cornish Hall. Last time she had gone that way, she reminded herself sadly, she hadn't yet met the doctor; now she couldn't imagine what life was going to be like without him. Very dull, she concluded and sad and purposeless as well, but it would be better when he had gone away and she had no chance of seeing him any more, and probably once he had returned to his own country Hilary would forget him. The thought that her cousin might be serious this time struck her with the suddenness of lightning and rooted her to the spot. It needed very little imagination to visualise a future in which her cousin triumphed as a lovely bride with herself trailing down the aisle behind her, no doubt in a gorgeous hat like Anne's, and in the course of time being given frequent invitations to Doesburg so that she could mind the children while Hilary and a doting husband explored the world together. It didn't bear thinking of;

she almost ran back to the comfort of Nanny and the nursery and tea.

"Hot buttered toast," said Nanny. "You make it, Miss Arabella, and I'll make the tea."

It was pleasant sitting before the old-fashioned fireplace, toasting bread on the brass fork which had always hung on the wall by the fire. Nanny waited until the toast had been eaten and second cups of the strong tea she favoured had been poured. "And now, Miss Arabella, I'll hear what there is to hear," she pronounced in a no-nonsense voice.

And Arabella told her, right from the beginning, and when she had finished the rather jumbled account of the accident and the doctor's house and the children, all woven round a perpetually recurring doctor, she said sadly: "You see, Nanny, I haven't a chance. I told you that – do you remember? Only it didn't seem to matter then because I never liked the men Hilary liked. But now it's different."

"Mr. Right," said Nanny in a vibrant voice, and nodded her head vigorously and with great satisfaction.

"Yes, he is – for me, but you see, Nanny, I'm not the girl he wants, though I did begin to think that he liked me a little. But not any more – and besides, Hilary has told him some silly nonsense about Bertie, though I'm not sure what." Two tears ran down her cheeks and she sniffed, and just as she used to do when she was a little girl, she buried her head in Nanny's lap.

"Nothing like a good cry," observed Nanny soothingly as she stroked the mousy topknot, and she was right; after a few minutes Arabella sat up again, mopped her face, and declared herself to feel much better and even suggested a third cup of tea. She was on the point of pouring it when there was a tap on the door and she put the teapot down again.

"Oh, Nanny, don't let anyone in, I look so awful!"

Nanny surveyed her. "Not awful, dearie, just a girl who's been crying. Turn your back and we'll see who it is."

The doctor stood in the doorway. He said with grave courtesy: "You must forgive me; I saw the light under the door and I guessed it was the nursery and I remembered. . . ." His eyes flickered briefly towards Arabella's hunched shoulders.

Nanny's small sharp eyes had missed nothing of him. "Come in, young man, since you are here," she invited him in a voice which brooked no refusal. "You would like a cup of tea."

He walked slowly towards them. "Very much, Miss Bliss, but perhaps. . . ?" He looked again at Arabella, staring into the fire, her back towards him.

"Sit down," said Nanny, just as though he had said nothing at all. "Miss Arabella shall make you some toast – proper toast, not that nasty stuff out of a toaster." She waited until Arabella had speared a slice of bread and held it to the glowing coals, then went to the old-fashioned dresser and fetched a cup and saucer and plate.

The doctor sat himself down, a little to one side of Arabella but behind her still, and when she asked in a small voice if he liked plenty of butter, replied with easy friendliness that really buttery toast was one of his favourite foods.

Nanny poured his tea, expressed her approval of his partiality for wholesome food, gave him three lumps of sugar when he asked for them, and asked: "Well, and did you enjoy your day, young man?"

He didn't quite answer her question, but: "The country around here is delightful – we went to the coast." He glanced at Arabella's rigid back. "This toast is delicious," he added, with so much enthusiasm that she picked up the toasting fork again.

"Shall I do you another piece?"

"Please." His quiet gaze took in the cosy, shabby room. "How peaceful it is here."

Nanny nodded contentedly. "Always has been and always will be while I'm here," she stated. "I doubt if you've known anything like it in those foreign parts." Her tone conjured up Whirling Dervishes, cave dwellers and multitudes of rough people who had never eaten buttered toast or enjoyed the privilege of speaking the English language.

The doctor made a small sound which might have been a chuckle and Arabella said hastily: "Nanny dear, the doctor lives in a lovely old house as peaceful as this one – it's beautiful there and very – very civilised."

The doctor's voice was very quiet. "How nicely put, Arabella," and she, forgetful of her blotchy, tear-stained face, turned round to look at him. "You have a lovely home," she assured him. "The people who have lived in it must have been happy. . . ."

He smiled. "I believe that too, only it is a little empty, isn't it? It needs children – the house came alive while Sally and Billy were there, and. . . ." He left the sentence unfinished, took the toast she offered him and began to munch.

"Where did you go today?" he asked presently.

"For a walk." She had turned her face away again.

"Alone?"

"Yes."

Nanny spoke unexpectedly. "Don't you think Hilary is just about the prettiest girl you've ever seen?" she wanted to know.

"Undoubtedly." His voice was bland.

"Such a lovely child she was," went on Nanny, ignoring Arabella's surprised look, "and clever too. Highly thought of at that hospital, so I'm told. We saw her on the telly the day those poor children went to Holland; talking to a man from the B.B.C. she was, saying how she doted on them. They said she was in charge of the bus, but of course that was a mistake. People make mistakes sometimes. I didn't see you, Miss Arabella."

"I went to find something for Sister Brewster just as they started filming," said Arabella uneasily. "It was natural that the reporter should get confused."

"I was confused myself the first time I set eyes on her," stated the doctor cheerfully. "I imagine she has that effect on everyone – even a confirmed middle-aged bachelor such as myself."

Nanny gave him a shrewd look. "The older you are,

the harder you fall," she informed him sternly, "just so long as it's the right one. But there, I can see there's no need to give advice where there's no need for it." She got to her feet. "There's that apple chutney in the kitchen. I'll be back in a jiffy, but you're welcome to stay as long as you like, Doctor."

The doctor ushered her out of the door and closed it behind her.

"And now you may tell me why you were crying."

"I wasn't c-cry ... well," Arabella felt peevish, "I suppose I can cry if I want to."

"I would rather you didn't," he said mildly. The very mildness of his voice stirred the peevishness to rage.

"It's none of your business! Oughtn't you to find Hilary? She'll wonder where you are."

"Probably. I had thought ... I had been looking forward to a talk with you."

"What about?" she snapped, her mind full of Hilary and Nanny being so unkind – why had she said all those nice things about her cousin?

"There is no use in asking you to come back with me tomorrow evening?"

Arabella ignored the wheedling tones. "None at all," she told him in a high artificial voice. "I don't want to go back until I must."

The doctor got to his feet. "No, of course not. Will you thank Miss Bliss for her delightful tea? I shall see you later, I have no doubt."

He took himself quietly off, leaving her sitting there without saying a word in reply. She was still staring at the fire when the door opened again and this time it was Hilary.

"There you are – I met Gideon on the stairs. What a charmer he is, Bella. I expect he thought you'd been left out – we didn't mean to stay away all day, but we were enjoying ourselves so much, and I told him you wouldn't mind, because of Bertie."

Arabella said heatedly: "That was a rotten low-down thing to say, Hilary! I haven't got him – I hate him, you know I do."

Her cousin's eyes sparkled. "I know, love, but you see, Gideon doesn't know that, he thinks you're quite happy – with Bertie. That leaves him free to take me out all he wants without feeling mean about it." She sat down in Nanny's chair. "I could fall for him, Bella – all that money, and so good-looking." She stared at Arabella. "What a pity it wasn't I who went on that wretched trip," she ruminated. "I would have had him hooked by now."

Arabella winced. "What about Mr. Thisby-Barnes?" she wanted to know coldly.

Hilary shrugged. "Oh, he's getting too serious – wants a divorce. Besides, he's getting to be a bore."

Arabella persisted: "But you made me go on to the trip because you wanted to go out with him so much!"

Her cousin eyed her with a kind of tolerant contempt. "Really, darling, you're what Nanny would call a green girl, aren't you? I suppose when you fall in love, it will be for ever and ever." She yawned and got to her feet. "Well, Gideon's taking me out to dinner – he asked if

134

you'd come to, but I told him not to suggest it to you because you were spending the evening with Bertie – you don't mind, do you?" She tripped to the door, not noticing Arabella's dumbfounded face. "Don't be surprised to find that we're engaged by the time we get back – I work fast once I've made up my mind, and Gideon's a walk-over." She saw Arabella's face at last. "You don't need to look like that, Bella – I'll be an awfully good wife – why not, with all the furs and clothes and jewels he's going to give me."

"Going to give you?" asked Arabella, breathless.

"Silly – he doesn't know that yet. 'Bye."

Arabella didn't move for quite some minutes, but when she did she got up briskly, went to her room, packed her case in minutes, rammed on the mackintosh and went back to the nursery. Nanny Bliss was back in her chair again, knitting. She raised her eyes briefly as Arabella went in, settled her spectacles more firmly and said: "You're going back, Miss Arabella? Did they telephone for you?"

"Yes – yes, Nanny. Aunt's out, isn't she, fetching the twins – I've just time to get to the station – I've got a taxi coming. Please will you tell her? They're – they're short of s-staff."

She kissed the old lady; if she had had a little more time she would have asked her why she had talked to the doctor as she did, but she had to get away from the house before Hilary or the doctor came downstairs. "I'll be back," she said uncertainly, not caring much whether she did or not. She would have to go to Wickham's because she had nowhere else to go; perhaps if she could think up something to tell Miss Trenchard, she would be able to go on duty in the morning.

She whiled away the dull journey, thinking up a suitable story.

CHAPTER SEVEN

IT seemed unlikely that Miss Trenchard would believe the cock-and-bull story Arabella had dredged up from a mind which could think only of Gideon van der Vorst. Certainly her various friends did not; she gave the vaguest of answers to their questions, and it was only after they had gone to their rooms and she was left sitting on Anne's bed, ostensibly to hear from that young lady's own lips of the success of the bridesmaid's hat, and the more feminine details of the wedding, that she divulged some, at any rate, of the truth.

Anne heard her out with sympathy. "Well, ducky," she said finally, "there's nothing you can do, is there? I mean, we all know what your cousin's like. Your only hope is that she'll get tired of him as quickly as she got tired of our Mr. Thisby-Barnes, and then you might be able to pick up the pieces."

"I have no wish to pick up the pieces," stated Arabella flatly. "I don't think I want to see him again – not ever."

"Well, you'll have to if Hilary gets him," advised her friend, "unless you go to the ends of the earth – and you haven't got your Finals yet."

Arabella got off the bed, brushed back her curtain of hair with an impatient hand and said: "Oh, well, there's always work. Is Men's Surgical busy?"

"Up to its eyes and overflowing, and that wretched Smithers is staffing."

Arabella yawned. "Oh, lord – she hates me, too. I'd better get some sleep, I suppose."

She wandered off to her room and got into bed, but didn't sleep at all.

Anne had been right; Men's Surgical was overflowing, with beds down the middle and the up patients sleeping out in less busy wards and having to be made comfortable for the day when they returned to spend their waking hours in the day room. Arabella, glad to have so much work to do that she had no time to think, went from patient to patient, doing dressings, escorting those destined for the theatre or X-Ray, and fetching them back again when the surgeon had dealt with them. In this work she was ceaselessly harried by Staff Nurse Smithers, a bespectacled young woman, very full of her own worth, and brimming over with self-importance, both of which virtues prevented her from doing her share of the work on the ward. She had an ingratiating manner however with her superiors, and was generally supposed by them to be an excellent staff nurse, who would one day make a good Ward Sister. None of her colleagues on the ward subscribed to this view; they disliked her and made no secret of the fact, even while they were forced to do as she told them.

Long before the day was over, Arabella was almost regretting her impulsive flight; she went off duty at last, too weary to do more than kick off her shoes and sprawl on her bed, drinking strong tea with those of her friends who were also off duty, until it was time to go to supper. But at least she slept that night, and the following morning woke to the realization that Hilary would have returned the night before and sooner or later she would meet her somewhere about the hospital. She would have to listen to her cousin's triumph, and that would be the least of it.

Arabella, kept unceasingly on the go by the horrible Smithers, prayed feverishly that she wouldn't have to meet Hilary – not just yet, anyway. And in a way her prayers were answered, for when she did encounter her cousin, she was bringing a patient back from theatre and was unable to stop. All Hilary could say was: "Bella, such a heavenly time – I'll tell you all about it." She had been laughing and was prettier than ever. Arabella, intent on her patient, who showed a nasty tendency to stop breathing, could do no more than nod her head. She wasn't off until eight o'clock that evening; Hilary would be sure to be going out – with Gideon, perhaps? It gave her a day's respite from hearing the news she wanted with all her heart never to hear.

She didn't see Hilary all the next day either. Private Patients was in the opposite wing of the hospital; unless they deliberately sought one another out, they might not meet for days. By the end of her fourth day back, Arabella had made up her mind to seek Hilary out. She wasn't off until eight o'clock and perhaps Hilary would be out, but at least she could go along to her room and find out, and if she was she could ask her about Gideon, because now she knew that if she didn't get him out of her mind, life was going to be difficult. If she knew . . . she wrenched her mind away from her own thoughts and went along to the dressings room, where Staff Nurse Smithers was waiting to chivvy her.

Hilary was in her room when Arabella went along after eight o'clock to see her, but when she caught sight of her cousin she said impatiently: "Oh, darling, not now. I've a date and I'm already late for it."

"With Gideon?" asked Arabella, trying to sound casual.

"Lord, no, more's the pity, for he would have taken me somewhere decent. No, I'm going out with that wretched Andrews man. I stood him up last week, and I can't do it again – besides, it will do Gideon good – it would never do for him to suppose there was no competition." She smiled at her reflection.

"Didn't he ask you to marry him?" asked Arabella in a kind of calm despair that turned to sudden hope as she realized what her cousin had said. The hope didn't last, her heart dropped to her feet again at Hilary's careless: "I fended him off for a few days – I'm not going to be too easy." She turned her head this way and that, studying her face, and her eyes met Arabella's in the mirror. "Do you like him, Bella?"

With a great effort Arabella managed not to stammer. "He's very kind and wonderful with children."

"Oh, stuff," said Hilary impatiently. "Didn't you get to know him at all? Didn't he . . . ? Not that you'd know." Her eyes narrowed. "Or would you, Bella?"

"No, I wouldn't," said Arabella, marvelling at her

140

powers of deception and thinking guiltily and with delight of the lovely time she had spent beside the doctor while they drove round the Dutch countryside, and the delights of exploring Arnhem with him. At least she had memories and Hilary would never know of them. She turned to go. "Is everything all right at home?" she asked.

"I imagine so. Nanny didn't feel well – very crabby she's getting. Father should pension her off."

Arabella looked at her cousin in horror. "But he couldn't! Nanny has been with us all her life, she's not old – it would kill her. And where would she go?"

Hilary shrugged her shoulders. "Who cares? Zip me up, Bella, before you go, will you?"

An unsatisfactory conversation, Arabella decided as she went back to her side of the Home. She would have to find out about Nanny, whom she dearly loved, and she must try even harder to forget Gideon – a resolution which largely accounted for a wakeful night.

It was theatre day again – Sir Justin Gold had a list as long as his arm and a heavy one at that; they would all be kept on their toes for the entire day. And her off duty had been changed; she was to go off at six, a circumstance she had that girl Smithers to thank for, because Smithers had discovered that there would be too much work to do if she were left on the ward with three junior nurses. With Arabella there as well she would be able to retire into Sister's office and leave Arabella to get on with it. Arabella grumbled half-heartedly, not really caring. She had no plans for the evening, but she could always find someone who would go to the cinema with her, she supposed. She bustled efficiently through her busy day, and when six o'clock came went off the ward thankfully.

She was half way down the stairs when she met Gideon coming up. It was impossible to avoid him; one simply did not turn tail and run, even if one felt like it — besides, her feet were aching. She slowed her pace and wished him a prim good evening. "Hilary's on the other wing," she told him helpfully.

"Hullo. Yes, I know, thank you. But had you forgotten our date for this evening? Are you off duty now? If so, we could go straight away."

Arabella had quite forgotten Mrs. Burns. Now she said, still determined to be of help at all costs: "Oh, dear, I'd forgotten! Anyway, I'm sure you don't want to waste time on that now. I'll go — I can get her address, I've got it written down somewhere. Then you'll be free to. . . ."

"To what?" his voice was cold.

"Why, go out," she faltered.

He was standing on the step below her, so that she didn't have so far to look up into his face, and peeped at it now and was taken aback to see how austere it was. Why was he angry? she wondered.

"What makes you think that I wish to go out?" he asked silkily.

"Well, don't you?" she countered, aware that it was a weak reply but not knowing what else to say.

"I was looking forward to an evening out," he told her, still silkily. "You know, Hilary told me that you regarded me as a middle-aged man, and I didn't believe her, but I see that I was mistaken. What is more, it seems probable that you don't like me sufficiently to bear with my company for an hour or so." He smiled at her, a coldly remote smile which struck chill into her bones and made her cry out:

"That's not true, it's not — n-not a w-word of it. You m-must believe me. And how c-could I s-suppose you to be a m-middle-aged man when you aren't? And I do like you. Oh, please don't be angry, I couldn't b-bear it. . . ."

She stopped, aware that her tongue, usually so tardy with its speech, had run away with itself. But to good purpose, it seemed; the ice had gone, his blue eyes were warm again. His voice was warm too.

"I'm sorry I was angry — I'm not any more — only why are you so anxious to pair me off with Hilary?"

She remembered what Hilary had said. "Well, she told me . . . that is, you mustn't mind her going out with Mr. Andrews; she doesn't like him very much, only she had promised him and she stood him up last week. She didn't mean you to quarrel about it . . . perhaps you could take her out tomorrow evening instead."

He was staring at her with an expressionless face. "Tomorrow evening I shall be back in Doesburg."

Her wide mouth curled into a smile. "And George and Crosby and Tatters and the kittens will be there waiting for you, and Emma will have made a fruit cake

143

for your tea." She drew a breath which was almost a sigh.

"Will you think of me there?"

She nodded a rather wispy head. "Oh, yes, of course."

"Friends again?" he wanted to know then, and when she said instantly: "But we never weren't," he added, "Then will you come and see Mrs. Burns?"

"Yes, of course. I'll be about twenty minutes."

She scrambled out of her uniform, bathed, did her face and hair, decided on the velveteen pinafore dress, covered it with a coat, and raced from her room. In the bottom corridor she met Doreen.

"Where's the fire?" asked her friend. "You're all dressed up. Why?"

Arabella paused long enough to say: "I'm going out – with Doctor van der Vorst," and heartened by her friend's cry of "Attagirl!" sped to the entrance.

The Bentley was there; as she got in she rushed into conversation, suddenly shy. "Do you always bring the car with you?" she wanted to know, and was told gravely that yes, he did, because it was more convenient than going by plane. "I like to go where I want when I want," her companion explained, "and now – will you guide me? I'm not sure where Waltham Green is."

"Well, it's Fulham," she wrinkled her brow in thought. "If we get into the Brompton Road and then into the Fulham Road – I believe it's somewhere near the Broadway."

"Good enough," declared the doctor unworriedly.

"We can always ask as we go, just so long as we don't waste time."

She had no reply to this damping remark, only sat silent beside him, wishing that she hadn't been fool enough to dress up in the pinafore outfit. He had no intention of prolonging their evening and he wouldn't even notice . . . thank heaven that her coat covered it completely.

"You're very quiet," observed her companion, turning the Bentley into Long Acre and traversing the brightly lighted streets of theatreland. "Have you had a busy day?"

Arabella replied stiffly that yes, she had been busy, and then, because she could think of nothing else to say, became silent again.

"Now what have I said," mused her companion aloud, "that could have turned you into a polite block of ice? Do you prefer not to visit Mrs. Burns, after all? I took it for granted that you would do so, but perhaps that was over-hasty of me."

"I shall be glad to talk to Mrs. Burns."

"Then it is I. . . . Ah, I have it, you've reversed your decision to be friends again."

"I haven't," protested Arabella hotly. "It's you, making such a thing about me coming with you and then declaring that we mustn't waste time."

She drew a loud breath, aware that she was being extremely childish and not caring in the least. "I'm aware that I'm dull company, but it was you who insisted upon me coming with you, and you could at least pretend."

They were passing Harrod's. The doctor slowed the car, drew in before its imposing doors and stopped.

"You can't park here," Arabella pointed out crossly.

"I know. Arabella, had it crossed your very feminine mind that if I had not wished to bring you with me this evening, I had no need to do so? After all, you ran out on me, didn't you? tearing back to Wickham's on one of the flimsiest excuses I have ever been expected to believe in my life. I could have washed my hands of you and not bothered to keep our date. And the reason I didn't wish to waste time was a simple one: I thought we might have dinner together after we have seen Mrs. Burns."

It was unfortunate that Arabella saw in this remark nothing more than a polite desire to make amends. She said far too quickly: "How kind – but I particularly want to be back at Wickham's at half past eight."

"A previous engagement?" he prompted gently.

"Yes." The stammer was back with a vengeance. "Yes, I've p-promised s-somebody."

As she had – to put up Anne's hair for the party she was going to when she got off duty; that this was a task which any of her friends might have undertaken was a point she ignored.

"Ah, well, there's nothing more to be said, is there?" The doctor's voice was so smooth that she gave him a suspicious glance which he met limpidly. "How is Bertie?"

He had started the car once more and they were going down the Fulham Road. Arabella turned to look at the doctor, her mouth slightly open, her eyes round. "How ever did you know he'd telephoned?" she wanted to know. It had only been a request for the address of someone Arabella knew who had some setter puppies for sale. "He telephoned this afternoon – so awkward, too, because I had no time to talk to him properly – not on operation day, you know ... such a waste of time. ..."

The doctor remained silent, which didn't surprise her. Bertie was a dull topic of conversation, and she abandoned him cheerfully. "It's here we have to turn off, I believe – I'll ask that fat man leaning on those railings, shall I?"

The doctor drew up obligingly, while Arabella received directions. She was on the point of relaying these to her companion when he interrupted her gently. "Don't bother, I think I have them well enough," he assured her, and turned the car down a side street.

"You must have a splendid memory and be awfully clever," Arabella told him. "After all, you're a foreigner, and he spoke quite shockingly."

"I agree that I'm a foreigner, but I begin to think that I'm not clever at all, dear girl. I don't much care for this neighbourhood – these rows of houses. ..."

"Well, people have to live somewhere. I daresay Mr. Burns was quite happy here, poor man."

They stopped before a small red brick house, one of a row, very neat and tidy as to curtains and paintwork, and got out and knocked on its narrow front door. The girl who opened the door was brown-haired, with mild blue eyes and a chubby face. Arabella thought her to be about fifteen years old. She looked at them without much curiosity when the doctor asked if her mother was at home.

The girl nodded and called over her shoulder: "Mum, here's two people 'ere ter see yer."

Mrs. Burns, when she appeared, was an elderly version of her daughter, she too, looked at them without much interest. She said "Evening," in a friendly enough voice, though.

"You must be wondering who we are," began Doctor van der Vorst, at his most reassuring. "This young lady, Miss Birch, was beside your husband in the bus when he died, and I came upon the scene shortly after. I telephoned you at the time, if you remember, and I am sure that you have been told a good deal by letter, but we thought, having been there, you might like to know as much as possible about your husband."

Mrs. Burns opened the door a little wider. "Come in," she said eagerly. "We've bin 'oping we'd 'ear more – yer know 'ow it is; nice letter and all that, but it ain't the same – no one knew nothing about Bill's last moments."

Her eyes filled with tears as she led the way to the small front room, stiffly furnished, very clean and almost never used. Arabella perched on an uncomfortable chair and watched the doctor lower himself with caution into a fireside chair which creaked ominously as it took his weight. Mrs. Burns settled herself between them, offered tea and sent the girl to get it. " 'E didn't suffer none?" she asked. "That's what I want ter know most of all."

The doctor glanced at Arabella. "He couldn't have

148

known a thing about it," she stated positively. "I noticed the bus wasn't being steered properly, but that was only seconds before Mr. Burns died. Only a few minutes before that he had been talking to me about the country we were passing through; he was perfectly all right then, Mrs. Burns. He seemed to be enjoying himself, and he was so sweet with the children and the greatest help to us. We all liked him very much."

Mrs. Burns wiped away a few more tears. "Now that's a real comfort ter me, miss. You're the little nurse 'e wrote about. 'E sent a card from that place where you spent the night. 'E said there was two nurses, an old duck 'oo did nothing, and a little dear wot worked herself ter string – that's you, miss. And glad I am that 'e 'ad such good company."

Arabella went pink. "Well, th-that's very n-nice of you t-to say so." She turned rather desperately to the doctor. "Doctor van der Vorst saw the accident, you know, and went straight to Mr. Burns."

Mrs. Burns nodded, her eyes on the doctor, who had sat silent in his flimsy chair. "Now yer can tell me, Doctor, did 'e die sudden like – not knowing, I mean?"

The tea had arrived. The girl gave them each a cup and then sat down with hers beside Arabella. The tea was richly brown and liberally laced with condensed milk. Arabella, aware, after living in the doctor's household, that while not a fussy man he expected and obtained the best of food and drink, correctly prepared, watched him as he swallowed the bitter brew with an inscrutable face, pausing after the first sip to compliment

149

the daughter of the house upon the excellence of her tea-making.

"Shirley makes a nice cuppa," explained her mother with pride, a remark to which he replied with a smile before emptying his cup.

"Now about your husband," he began, "it is of course a very painful subject, but I quite understand that you wish to know as much as possible, and I will certainly tell you all I know."

He did it very nicely, saying nothing of the more harrowing details but painting a picture of the whole unhappy episode which could not but comfort his listeners. Arabella listened to his unhurried voice and thought he was the most wonderful man in the whole world, and if Mrs. Burns' opinion didn't quite match hers, it was certainly a warm one, for her thanks, when he had finished, were almost embarrassing. It was as they were preparing to leave that the doctor suggested to Arabella that she might help Shirley take the cups and saucers to the kitchen, and interpreting his suggestion as a wish to be left alone with Mrs. Burns, she retired to the small kitchen at the back of the house, and dried while Shirley washed, enjoying a little chat at the same time. When they returned to the sitting room it was to find the doctor bidding Mrs. Burns goodbye.

"A brave little woman," he remarked as he found his way unerringly back to the Fulham Road. "Thank you for coming, Arabella. I hope your evening won't be spoilt; it's only just eight o'clock, you should be in plenty of time." He gave her a brief glance. "What is it to be? Dinner somewhere or a theatre?"

If only he knew! thought Arabella; she had a fleeting vision of herself back-combing Anne's hair into a state of perfection, then retiring to bed with a book – she would have missed supper. "It's t-to be a s-surprise," she told him. "I l-like surprises." She peered from the window. "Oh, here's Long Acre already." She had tried to make her voice sound excited and was rewarded by a grunt from the doctor and silence until he had eased the Bentley through the gates and stopped at the hospital entrance.

"Thank you for taking me," she told him awkwardly, her fanciful account of the evening before her lying heavy on her. "I'm sure Mrs. Burns was very glad – I know I should have been." She remembered something. "Why did you want to see her alone?" She looked at him as she spoke and was surprised to see embarrassment in his face. "Whatever was it that I wasn't supposed to hear?"

He shrugged his shoulders. "I could tell you to mind your own business, my girl, but that would be unkind, wouldn't it? Just take my word for it that it didn't concern you." He gave her a look which bordered upon the haughty, daring her to say more, so that of course she declared: "I shall guess – it couldn't have been anything to do with Shirley, she would have told me – and nothing to do with Mr. Burns' death because I was there, anyway, wasn't I?" She frowned, unheeding of his quiet: "You'll be late, Arabella."

The frown cleared. "I know," she said suddenly.

"You gave her some money, didn't you?" and when he didn't answer: "Didn't you?"

"I am forced, after all, to tell you to mind your own business, Arabella."

"Pooh, it is my business. Oh, Gideon, you are a dear – I know one isn't supposed to think of sordid things like money when someone dies, but it must be far worse when you're poor ... all the worry...." She sniffed, wishing most earnestly to cry, and was instantly brought to her senses by her companion's matter-of-fact: "For God's sake, don't start weeping, and if you ever dare to so much as hint to anyone, I will personally strangle you!"

Arabella blew her nose and said coldly: "There's no need to get violent, Doctor."

"You called me Gideon a few moments ago, and I was a dear."

She had to laugh then. "Oh, you are absurd – it was a f-figure of speech.

"I hope you h-have a n-nice trip back," she said when he had helped her out of the car. Her voice was shaking a little at the thought of not seeing him; if he came to visit Hilary, and she was sure that he would, she would take care not to be there.

His reply was cool. "Thank you, I see no reason why I shouldn't." He added deliberately: "Will you tell Hilary that I shall hope to see her again? No, on second thoughts, I'll telephone her." He smiled suddenly, his voice full of unexpected warmth. "Enjoy your evening, little Arabella – you deserve all the happiness in the world."

She gave him her hand and found her voice. "Oh, and so do you," she told him earnestly, "and I do hope you will find it." There was a pause while she struggled with the return of the stammer. "G-goodbye," she managed at last, and flew through the doors, not looking back.

Anne was waiting, her head held rigid by the complexity of rollers necessary to achieve the elaborate hairstyle she had decided upon for the party. She took one look at Arabella's face and asked: "What's up, Bella? You look shattered – feeling rotten?"

Arabella shook her head. "I'm fine," she managed a smile. "Let's get that hair done."

She had been working on it for several minutes when Anne said:

"You've been out, haven't you? With that doctor of yours."

"He's n-not m-mine," muttered Arabella, fiercely thrusting in pins. "He's gone, back to Holland."

"What about Hilary?"

Arabella spoke through a mouthful of grips. "I d-don't know – at least, she t-told me she was holding him off, b-because it w-wouldn't be g-good for him t-to get his own way." She sniffed. "He said he was going to telephone her."

"Anyone can talk," Anne's voice was comforting. "What happened this evening, ducky?"

"Nothing." Arabella gave a brief account of the evening's activities. "I t-told him I had an important engagement, and he d-didn't seem to mind," she added forlornly.

Anne said "Um" thoughtfully, and Arabella, not wishing to talk about herself any more, concentrated frowningly upon her friend's hair. Neither of them mentioned the doctor again.

Two days later Arabella saw Hilary on her way through the hospital and this time there was time to stop and talk for a few minutes. It was her cousin who mentioned Gideon first.

"Have you heard from him?" she demanded pettishly. "He's just gone off without a word. Of course, it was my own silly fault, but I was so sure. . . ." She broke off, frowning. "He's paying me back in my own coin." she decided. "He'll turn up one day, and this time I'll make sure of him." She grinned in anticipation.

"Do you love him?" asked Arabella, carefully careless.

Hilary shrugged. "Oh, he's great fun and rich and his manners are super; he's very good-looking too – it shouldn't be hard to make him happy." She smiled thoughtfully. "Just think of all that money, Bella!"

Arabella had clamped her teeth down on her tongue for fear it should say the things she wanted to say, and Hilary should guess. With an effort she spoke of something else. "I telephoned home about Nanny – she's still not very well. I'm going home on my days off. Sister gave me Saturday and Sunday for this week and

154

Monday and Tuesday for next, so that I can stay for a bit."

Hilary wasn't very interested. "The end of the week . . . I want to do some shopping on Saturday. I shan't bother to go home – you know what it will be, fussing round Nanny and having to keep an eye on the twins." She shuddered. "You go – you're so useful, Bella. Buy Nanny some flowers or something, will you? I'll pay you some time." She smiled, an easy smile which meant nothing at all, and tripped off down the corridor, leaving Arabella vaguely worried about Nanny and even more worried about Gideon because Hilary didn't love him at all.

It was Smithers, smiling a mean little smile, who told her on Friday afternoon that Hilary had been fetched by the Dutch doctor everyone was talking about – he'd taken her home; she had it on the best authority from one of the staff nurses on the Private Wing. Staff Nurse Grey had been livid because Sister Birch wasn't due for a day off until Saturday, but she had gone just the same, leaving the staff nurses to split her duties between them. "She gets away with murder, does Sister Birch," commented Smithers nastily.

Arabella agreed silently, but family loyalty was strong. "You haven't any r-right to m-make spiteful r-remarks like that," she declared hotly. "Probably my cousin had to go home on urgent business. . . ."

"Ha – you must be joking, Birch, unless urgent business is twisting that doctor round her thumb until he finds himself married to her."

Arabella choked. "H-how dare you!" she exploded. "You're nothing b-but a spiteful c-cat! I c-can't stand the s-sight of you!"

She had been laying up a dressing tray. Now she picked it up, dumped it into her senior's arms and walked out of the dressing room. And Staff Nurse Smithers, who for once knew that she had gone too far with the usually mild-tempered Arabella, meekly followed her, the tray still in her hands; she even did the dressing of the patient for whom it had been intended.

Strong emotion, Arabella had discovered during the last few weeks, was more exhausting than a hard day's work; she packed a case when she got off duty, put her clothes ready for the morning so that she might catch an early train, had her bath, washed her hair, plaited it neatly for the night and got into bed. She hadn't wanted any supper, she put out the light and curled up and closed her eyes. She opened them almost immediately because someone was knocking thunderously on the door, and before she could say come in, had done so and switched on the light as well.

"Whether you want to come or not," said Gideon from the doorway, "Nanny wants you. She's ill – you knew that, didn't you?"

She was sitting up in bed, her rope of hair over one shoulder.

"Yes, Hilary told me. . . ."

"And although you have days off you chose to stay so that you might go shopping." He sounded contemptuous.

156

She didn't know what to say – if he loved Hilary, he would never believe her if she told him the truth, and he must love Hilary very much, because here he was, coming to see her again. "You mustn't come here," she told him fiercely. "It's forbidden."

"Damn the rules! If you don't get up and dress, my girl, and be downstairs in five minutes from now, I'll come and dress you myself."

Arabella had her hand on the bedcovers. "Does Hilary know you've come back for me?"

"Yes. She didn't want me to come – indeed, she begged me not to – she said that she could manage Nanny very well by herself. She didn't wish to spoil your days off." Again the contempt in his voice, and furious anger too. "But Nanny begged me to fetch you."

"Get out of my room." Arabella spoke urgently. She would have to go with him; it would be of no use explaining that she had her train ticket ready for the morning; that it was Hilary who had wanted to go shopping. In fact, she thought wearily, tearing into her clothes, it wasn't any good explaining anything any more.

CHAPTER EIGHT

DURING their almost silent journey, Arabella was able, from the few remarks the doctor let fall from a grimly set mouth, to piece together the happenings which had led to his unorthodox visit to the Nurses' Home. He had been attending some meeting or other at Wickham's during the afternoon, and afterwards had happened to meet Hilary, who had poured out her tale of Nanny Bliss being ill and how she was going, by hook or by crook, to her home that very afternoon, so that she might nurse her. And when, he said bitingly, he had offered to take Arabella at the same time, he had been told that although she had days off and could be spared far more easily from the ward than could Hilary, she had told Hilary that she preferred to stay in London and do some shopping, whereupon he had suggested that they might go together and endeavour to persuade Arabella to change her mind, but Hilary had put forward the unselfish plea to leave the matter where it stood. It was only when he had seen Nanny Bliss for himself, went on the doctor austerely, and had realized how much she wished to see Arabella, that he had taken upon himself to return to London and fetch her.

"I cannot believe," he concluded with a remote coldness which took all the warmth from the car, "that you would grudge a few hours to someone who has been so good to you throughout her life."

"Believe what you like!" snapped Arabella, and then

subsided into numbed silence. Gideon seemed bent on seeing her in the worst possible light, and there would be no use in trying to make him do otherwise. She sat like a statue beside him, thinking with nostalgia of Doesburg and his home and the fun and laughter there had been in it. Her tight-lipped companion wasn't the same man; it astonished her that despite this she still loved him as deeply, indeed her love wove like a golden thread through her unhappiness, as strong and tough as a parachute cord. She sighed deeply and began to think what she would say to Hilary when she saw her. She was still wondering about this when they arrived at Little Dean House.

There were only a few lights burning, for it was late now. At the door she paused. "You're staying the night?"

"Yes," his voice was abrupt. He shut the door behind them and followed her across the hall towards the sitting room, where there was a lamp burning — someone was still up. Halfway there she remembered her case in the car and turned back to fetch it with such abruptness that she caught her handbag on the edge of a side table and let it fall to the ground, scattering half its contents, the ticket amongst them. She bent to snatch it up, only to have the doctor's hand close over her own, take it from her, and with great deliberation, scrutinize it for himself. When he handed it back, his brows were drawn together in thought.

"Arabella. . . ." he began, to be interrupted by Mrs. Birch coming from the sitting room.

She greeted them both with an air of harassment. "There you are, Arabella – now perhaps Nanny will settle down. So good of you, Gideon, going all that way to fetch my niece." She looked at Arabella and said with faint irritation: "I expected you sooner, you know. After all, I telephoned Hilary quite early in the morning and I'm sure you could have got leave to come home far more easily than poor Hilary with all her responsibilities."

Arabella muttered. Hilary had spun a pretty web, and she could see no way out of it; she could of course tell the truth, and much good that would do her. Her aunt wouldn't believe her, and Gideon, enthralled by Hilary, would regard her as no more than a spiteful teller of tales. When her aunt continued: "Perhaps you would go straight up to Nanny, Arabella, so that Hilary can have a few hours' rest," Arabella turned on her heel and went upstairs without even glancing at Gideon.

Nanny was in her own little room next to the nursery, looking small and frail in her narrow bed, with the oxygen cylinder beside it, and an array of medicine bottles and pill boxes on the little mantelshelf. She was asleep, but it was a troubled rest, with a good deal of tossing and turning. Hilary was curled up in a chair by the fire, deep in a magazine, but she looked up as Arabella went in and jumped to her feet.

"Thank God!" she said pettishly. "I'm just about fed up with sitting here doing nothing." She gave Arabella a sharp glance. "What did Gideon tell you?"

"The lies you told him." Arabella spoke in a whisper
160

too, which was an effort; she longed to use a voice as strong as her feelings.

Hilary flung a casual arm round her shoulders. "Oh, Bella, don't be ratty! It was just the chance I wanted – what luck bumping into him like that this afternoon. I've let him glimpse the dear little woman under my apparently useless exterior. And what does it matter what he thinks of you, anyway?" She went to the door. "There's nothing to do for Nanny – oxygen when she needs it, antibiotics at two o'clock and again at six. Usual nursing treatment and so forth." She made a bored face. "You'll find all clutter in the bathroom – drinks are on the table." She glanced towards the bed. "She should have gone into hospital, the tiresome old thing – I've told Daddy that when she's fit enough, he must get her moved into an old people's home."

Arabella looked at her cousin with horror. "But you can't! You said that before, and you just can't – this is her home, she's been here. . . ."

"You've said that before too, Arabella, and I daresay you'll repeat yourself over and over again, but it won't make the smallest difference. She's got double pneumonia, by the way – there's not the slightest reason why she shouldn't get over it."

She went away, closing the door very gently behind her, and Arabella went back to the bed. Nanny was awake. What was more, it was plain to see that she had heard their conversation. Arabella caught the old lady's hand in hers and said fiercely: "She was only joking, Nanny – of course you'll stay here."

"That's why I wanted you here, Miss Arabella – I guessed, you see – but you can't do anything about it." Nanny's voice was quavery and a bit thin, but there was no doubt that she was *compos mentis*. "They'll move me to one of those homes where no one wants you."

"They won't," declared Arabella. "Why, Nanny, you're only just a little over sixty, and I promise you that you shan't go into a home – I'll think of something, you see if I don't. Now I'm going to give you a drink and make you comfortable and you're going to sleep – you'll feel better in the morning."

Nanny submitted to Arabella's capable hands, muttering from time to time that the boot was on the other foot now, and did Miss Arabella remember sitting on her knee and having her face washed?

Arabella answered in a soothing way as she settled her patient for the night, and presently Nanny went to sleep and Arabella was able to pull up a chair and sit down close to the bed. She was sleepy herself by now, but there was no question of her leaving the old lady and no one had come to see if she needed anything. She hadn't expected that. She turned out the lights but for a shaded lamp by the chair, made up the fire and prepared to stay the night. Nanny's everlasting knitting lay on the chest of drawers. Arabella picked it up – socks for the twins; one was completed, the other half done; she began to turn the heel, the needles clicking an accompaniment to her busy thoughts. If her uncle intended to send Nanny away, she would have to do something about it. The obvious thing was to find a small flat or rooms close to

Wickham's and live out so that Nanny could live with her. Once she had finished her training she would be able to get a job at a smaller hospital in a provincial town where they would be able to make a life for themselves. She would have to work fast, though, and Nanny would have to get better quickly so that there would be no excuse to send her to hospital. Perhaps when she wakened they could have a little talk.

The quiet knock at the door surprised her. She got up and opened it soundlessly and found Gideon there. His eyes went past her into the quiet little room. "I was told that you had gone to bed."

"Hilary isn't here." Arabella's whisper was tart.

He took no notice at all of this but stretched out an arm and pulled the door to. "You didn't know that Nanny was so ill – Hilary didn't tell you." His eyes searched her tired face. "I'm right, am I not?"

She answered him in a haughty voice sadly at variance with her untidy hair and unmade-up face. "I don't want to talk about it. I'm going back to sit with Nanny."

"You've been on duty all day; you must have some sleep."

Her whisper was choked with temper. "And while I sleep, perhaps she'll be moved to hospital, and when she's better they'll put her in an old people's home. I won't leave her until she's well enough to come with me," she finished with wild inaccuracy.

He put his hands on her shoulders and kept them there, although she tried to shrug them away.

"Listen to me, Arabella – you will do as I say. You

163

will go to bed now and I will sit with Nanny, and I give you my word that no one shall take her away. You have every reason to be angry with me, but trust me in this. Perhaps in the morning it will be possible to sort this whole matter out."

She stared up at him. Even while boiling with rage against him, she trusted him too. "What about you?" she asked.

"I haven't been on duty all day," he pointed out in a matter-of-fact voice. "Tell me what there is to do."

She told him. "I'll be back by six," she added, "though I don't think you ought to. . . ."

"Probably you don't, Arabella." He gave her a gentle push. "Good night."

She hesitated. "But didn't you want to see Hilary?"

A muscle at the corner of his mouth twitched. "I don't remember saying that." He opened the door and disappeared into Nanny's room.

It was half past six when Arabella wakened. She was out of bed in a flash and bundled in her dressing gown, went quietly through the house to the invalid's room. Nanny was awake, looking pale and wan but decidedly better. Moreover, she was sipping a cup of tea, and the doctor, sitting comfortably in the chair by the bed, was having one with her.

He looked up as Arabella went in, said: "Hello – have some tea," and offered his chair.

"I overslept," explained Arabella, a little breathless. "I'm so sorry. Thank you very much for staying with Nanny – you must think me a very stupid sort of person, but now it's morning, it doesn't seem as bad."

"I don't think you stupid; it is I who have been stupid, and I agree wholeheartedly, now it is morning, it doesn't seem so bad."

Arabella had kissed Nanny Bliss and accepted a cup of tea. Now she perched on the end of the bed to drink it. "Where did you get it?" she asked.

"Miss Bliss was good enough to tell me where I might find the kitchen – after that it was merely a simple process of elimination. I'm handy around the house, you know."

The invalid gave a ghost of a chuckle. "You're a proper tease, young man. That was a nice chat we had, though."

"Oh, Nanny, you're better." Arabella gulped her tea and beamed with relief. "We'll have you as fit as a fiddle in no time. Does Doctor West come today?"

"Yes." The elderly face looked suddenly anxious, so that Arabella said briskly. "Good – he'll have you on your feet in a few days. Won't he?" She addressed the doctor, who said at once: "Undoubtedly – I can see no reason to doubt that." He got up and tidied the cups and saucers onto a tray, yawning prodigiously. "I don't think there is any need to mention that I have been here, do you? It might shake your aunt's sense of hospitality." He strolled to the door, looking very spruce although he needed a shave. "Good morning to you both."

Neither lady spoke for a few minutes after he had gone until Nanny, who appeared to have taken on a new lease of life, remarked: "A nice young man, Miss Ara-

bella, no one would ever know that he wasn't English."
High praise indeed from Nanny Bliss!

Arabella agreed with her as she started on the early
morning chores. Nanny was right. Gideon was nice;
more than that, he was wonderful and kind and deserved
the best from life – only the best for him was Hilary,
who didn't love him. She was aroused from her thoughts
by Nanny saying:

"He's still Mr. Right, isn't he, Miss Arabella?" and
was startled into replying:

"Oh, Nanny, yes!"

An hour later, with Nanny coaxed to take nourish-
ment and nicely settled against her pillows, Arabella
went to dress and go down to breakfast. Everyone was
already at table, even Hilary, looking more eye-catching
than ever. Arabella was greeted with slightly frosty kindness by her uncle and aunt, shouts of welcome by the
twins and a punctilious good morning from the doctor,
followed by general enquiries as to Nanny's condition,
although no one waited to hear her answer. It was Hilary
who said gaily; just as though they had parted the best
of friends the night before:

"Good old Bella, what should we do without you?
You look peaked, though, darling – are you starting a
cold? If you are, for heaven's sake keep away from me,
you know how I hate catching the beastly things."

She turned to Gideon, who, Arabella perceived,
looked as though he had slept the clock round and then
had a valet to dress him. "Gideon, Mother says you
have to go again this morning." She pouted prettily.

166

"I've hardly seen you. I know what I'll do – I'll come back with you to London. Perhaps we could have lunch?"

Her smile was enough to turn any man's head.

"That would be a pleasure, Hilary, but I thought that you would be remaining to look after Miss Bliss."

The smile cracked briefly and became whole again. "But there's no need now that Bella's here – she always was Nanny's pet and she can manage her far better than any of us." She laughed across the table at Arabella, but the sting was there. Just the same, Arabella went on eating her breakfast as though she hadn't been listening.

The doctor buttered a piece of toast and spread it with marmalade, his eyes intent upon it.

"They're dreadfully short-staffed on the Private Wing," confided Hilary. "If I go back today, it might help a little."

The doctor looked up briefly. "I thought of leaving in a couple of hours – will that suit you?"

"Perfectly." Hilary's smile was radiant. Arabella, watching from over the rim of her cup, saw the full force of it directed against Gideon – he must be completely dazzled, only if he was, he was holding his feelings well in hand.

He buttered more toast. "I want to go to the garage in the village before we leave. I could do that while you pack," he suggested.

He left the house half an hour later and drove off down the road to the village. Only he didn't go anywhere near the garage; he drove to the Rectory, where he enquired if he might see Mr. Bertie Palmer.

Bertie was finishing his breakfast and wasn't best pleased to have a caller at such an awkward hour, but he was curious to see this Dutch doctor his mother – a close friend of Mrs. Birch – had been so full of. He swallowed the rest of his coffee and strolled along to the sitting room, wondering what might be the object of such a visit.

His caller was standing by the french window, looking out on to the garden and blocking a good deal of the light from the room in consequence. It annoyed Bertie to discover that he was forced to look up quite a long way into his visitor's face, but all the same he said graciously:

"Good morning, Doctor – er – van der Vorst." He offered a limp hand as he spoke and had it so ruthlessly crushed in the doctor's large, firm grasp that he all but cried out.

"Good day to you, Mr. Palmer," answered the doctor with deliberation, eyeing his host with a disconcertingly steady gaze, while a peculiar expression passed over his calm features. It could have been tearing rage, followed swiftly by amusement and relief – it was hard to tell, and Bertie wasn't a discerning young man. He asked a little stiffly:

"You wished to see me?"

"Oh, indeed I do," replied the doctor, and now amusement plainly had the upper hand. "I have come to ask you a question which I hope very much you will not resent, coming as it does from a complete stranger."

Bertie assumed what he hoped was a worldly air and

tried not to look uneasy. "What's that?" he demanded.

The doctor's voice was very even. "Miss Arabella Birch – are you engaged to be married to her?"

Whatever question Bertie had expected, this certainly wasn't the one. He looked open-mouthed with astonishment at his visitor and said weakly:

"I say, wherever did you get that from?" His look changed to apprehension. "Bella? I wouldn't have her for a million pounds!" He caught the doctor's eye and something in it made him say hastily: "What I mean to say is, we've known each other since we were kids, but that doesn't mean to say. . . . Why, she's always telling me off, I can tell you – not my type at all, though the parents are always pushing us to be friends." His voice rose. "Why, she likes birds and small children and long walks in the rain – I pity the man who. . . ."

"Save your pity," counselled the doctor in a dangerously soft voice. "And thank you for your most enlightening answer. I'll bid you good morning."

Bertie ushered him out, trying to keep up with his enormous strides while he began and never finished a string of incoherent remarks, hardly noticing the pain as the doctor crushed his metacarpal bones once more and bade him a courteous goodbye. He stood on the step, watching the Bentley with envy, and then wandered back into the house, brooding over the peculiar ways of foreigners and nursing his aching hand.

Gideon drove slowly and in deep thought back to Little Dean House, where he walked silently through the hall and up the stairs, to knock on Nanny Bliss's door.

When he heard Arabella's voice inviting him to go in, he did so, barely glancing at her as he went to the bed. Nanny was awake, refreshed after a nap and a glass of warm milk which Arabella had just removed. Her visitor said composedly: "You're feeling better, aren't you? Do you suppose you feel well enough to continue our little talk for a few minutes?"

Nanny examined his face. "Private like?"

He nodded and then turned to Arabella, standing by the door with the milk. "You don't mind, Arabella? I want a few words with Miss Bliss before I go."

She didn't quite look at him. "No, of course I don't mind, but Doctor West will be here in a few minutes."

"Splendid." He opened the door for her and when she gave him a questioning look, told her blandly: "Miss Bliss and I share the same interests. I promise you I won't tire her." And as she went past him: "Arabella, I should like to talk to you before I go." He had put a hand on her arm, but she moved away and he took it away immediately.

"I don't think there will be time," said Arabella, suppressing a strong urge to burst into tears. "I'd rather not, if you don't mind."

"I do mind, but I won't press you. What I have to say to you cannot be said in a couple of minutes. But at least let me apologise."

The railway ticket, of course, and calling her names because she didn't want to see Nanny. "It's quite all right, thank you," she said, very polite and not stammering at all. "It was a perfectly natural mistake." She put

170

out a hand for him to take. "Perhaps you had better have your little chat with Nanny, or Doctor West will be here."

She went to her room and stayed there until she heard Doctor West's booming voice enquiring for her. He was in Nanny's room, and so, to her surprise, was Gideon. The two men stared at her as she went in, and she frowned a little, aware that she was hardly looking her best. Doctor West greeted her with a bluff: "There you are, Arabella. Everyone else is in the sitting room drinking sherry – why aren't you? You look as though you could do with it. What have you been doing to Nanny, eh? She's taken a decided turn for the better since I saw her yesterday – another couple of days should see her out of the wood. You will be here for that time, I gather? I'll get the district nurse to come over twice a day when you go, so that Nanny is well looked after."

Arabella had gone to stand by the bed. "Nanny can stay here? There'll be no need to send her to hospital?"

"No, nor anywhere else; set your mind at rest about that, Arabella. Go on with the antibiotics, will you, increase the diet – lots of fluids – and see that she swings her legs out of bed at least twice a day."

He patted her on the shoulder in fatherly fashion and made for the door, saying as he went: "Shall we have that little talk as we go down to the car?" And Gideon, who had uttered no word, followed him out.

"What have they got to talk about?" Arabella wanted to know, not really interested, but it was something to say, and if she didn't say something she would think

171

about Gideon; that he had gone without saying goodbye and she had no idea if or when she would see him again.

"Men," observed Nanny from her bed, "they don't go about things like a woman would." Which didn't answer the question at all. But Arabella was drawing up the next dose of Ledermycin and wasn't really listening.

Gideon made no attempt to see her before he went. She didn't see Hilary either, but she heard their goodbyes being said in the hall below, and went across the landing to watch them go. Hilary had on the new winter coat with its hood framing her lovely face. She looked pleased with herself, and so, Arabella saw to her sorrow, did Gideon.

She stayed for the remainder of her days off and had the satisfaction of seeing Nanny's steady improvement. Of her aunt and uncle she saw very little; at meal times, naturally enough, and for an hour in the evening, but beyond a kindly and rather vague interest in Nanny's health and their expressions of relief that Arabella was there to look after her, they took very little interest, her aunt's attention, at least, being settled for the moment upon Hilary and her gratifying conquest of the wealthy and more than presentable Gideon, although as her aunt remarked one evening as they sat together after supper: "I do wonder if we are perhaps a little premature in supposing dear Hilary is to marry Gideon. Perhaps I am unobservant, but I can't say that I have noticed anything in his manner towards her which suggests it. He drives her up and down to Wickham's, of that I'm aware, but only when she's asked him to do so. Possibly he's of a different nature from other men-friends she's had; they seemed to me to be always under foot."

Arabella didn't look up from her knitting. "The doctor's a busy man and he doesn't live in England," she volunteered in a colourless voice, "and he's n-not so very young."

"But so handsome," murmured her aunt, "and all that money – not that he's ever actually mentioned ... but that car and his clothes, and Hilary asked one of the registrars at Wickham's...." She frowned. "I hope Hilary will persuade him to come again soon – I did invite him, you know, but he seemed a little uncertain." She laughed. "Indeed, almost reluctant, but that is, of course, quite absurd."

Arabella went back to hospital the following day, with Nanny transferred to the kindly district nurse, who promised faithfully to let her know if Nanny should take a turn for the worse or didn't progress as she ought. And Arabella had begged a few minutes of Doctor West's time too, and outlined to him her plans about having Nanny to live with her. He had been very kind.

"Don't worry that little head of yours," he reassured her. "Nanny is in good hands, I promise you she won't be going to any homes for the aged, so don't rush into things. When do you take your Finals?"

"In about nine months' time."

"And what do you intend doing?"

She looked at him forlornly. "I d-don't know, Doctor West."

"What – no hidden ambition to set the nursing world
173

on fire?"

She shook her head. "No," she said seriously, "but I daresay I'll think of something – or something might happen," she finished vaguely.

"Indeed it might," he let out a cheerful bellow of laughter. "In the meantime don't worry about Nanny."

She got to Wickham's in the evening, too late for supper, which was a good excuse for a general whip-round for the purchase of fish and chips from the shop on the corner, while Arabella, not having been on duty like her hard-working colleagues, made the tea and collected mugs. Gossip was mostly shop; it nearly always was to start with. Only when the various operations, diagnoses, admissions and unfair treatment meted out on the part of various Ward Sisters had been discussed and sifted down to their very foundations did the talk turn to lighter subjects.

What did Arabella think of her cousin's conquest of the Dutch doctor? someone wanted to know, but before she needed to answer Anne spoke up:

"You know, everyone's talking about a conquest, but he doesn't look a bit smitten to me; just good-natured – I mean, what's so extraordinary about giving a girl a lift these days, especially when she asks for one? If he's in love with her, I'll eat my hat!"

There was an instant chorus of protest. "Not the bridesmaid's hat – it's far too gorgeous. Eat that awful thing you bought in Oxford Street and hated when you got it back here." And someone chimed in: "Arabella, talking of clothes, you've branched out, haven't you?

174

That pinafore dress and that gay mac – don't tell me it's the. . . ."

Arabella interrupted hastily: "Oh, I've got my eye on that bearded type in the Path Lab."

There was a scream of laughter as the party broke up to wash greasy fingers, wind hair into rollers and get to the bathrooms first, leaving Arabella and Anne together.

"Has he gone, Arabella? I mean, not to come back again?"

Arabella nodded. "As far as I know – he didn't tell me; he didn't say goodbye," she swallowed the tears in her throat. "He's not in love with Hilary, I think – dazzled, perhaps – who wouldn't be? I don't know any more, he's never given a hint . . . but she'll get him, you s-see if s-she d-doesn't." She sniffed, "I'll tell you what happened the other evening."

When she had finished Anne got off the bed and strolled to the dressing table to pick up her hair brush. "That was a rotten trick – do you suppose he saw through it when he picked up the ticket?"

"Perhaps, but what good would that do? He th-thinks I'm going to m-marry Bertie."

Her friend gave a snort of laughter. "If only he'd met him, he'd change his mind about that!" She wandered round the little room, brushing her hair. "Arabella, don't give up – oh, I know you'd never make a play for him, you're not like that. I don't suppose you know how – but don't give up."

Arabella started for the door. "I know that's good advice, but I don't think it's much use," she declared,

175

"but thanks for listening, all the same, Anne. Is Doreen back?"

Anne nodded. "And gone again — wangled another week's holiday — got herself engaged to some Scottish engineer. She sent her love and said be good."

"I never have the chance to be anything else," muttered Arabella bitterly, "but it's nice for her." She wandered off with a soft good night because the lights were out by now and the Home was quiet. She went to her room and got into bed; it was almost morning before she finally went to sleep.

Men's Surgical was full, because it was take-in week and there seemed to have been a burst of accidents in the neighbourhood. The fact that for once she was forced to do her share of the work had put Staff Nurse Smithers into a bad frame of mind. She pounced upon Arabella as soon as she appeared on the ward the next morning, gave her an impossible amount of work to do and then shadowed her for the entire morning to make sure that it was done.

"Look," said Arabella, thoroughly fed up, "if you got on with some of the dressings yourself instead of wasting time breathing down my neck, we might get finished."

Smithers glared at her. "I'll report you for rudeness!" she began.

"Oh, pooh to you," said Arabella; she had discovered that being in love with Gideon and knowing that it was hopeless had given her a don't-care attitude to life, which in the case of the wretched Smithers, had a highly salutary result. She was left in peace to get on with her work for the rest of the day, and indeed, during the days which followed she was allowed to get through her work with the minimum of interference.

She went home on her next days off and found Nanny much better; sitting in her chair by the nursery fire once more. They had tea together and Nanny, rather surprisingly, wanted to know how Hilary was getting on.

"I've only seen her twice," admitted Arabella. "She's a bit put out – I think because Doctor van der Vorst went back to Holland without s-saying anything."

"I daresay she was," commented Nanny dryly. "She'll have found other company, no doubt."

"Well, yes – there's a new Registrar on the Medical side – I expect she's lonely."

Nanny snorted. "And you, are you lonely, Miss Arabella?"

Arabella was on her knees, mending the fire. "Oh, Nanny, yes!"

CHAPTER NINE

SHE went back to Wickham's the next afternoon, ready for duty in the morning, and was in her room with several friends and acquaintances sharing the inevitable pot of tea after supper, when there was a knock on the door. There was a chorus of "Come ins" and Larissa's rather startled face peered in at the crowd of nurses in a variety of dress and undress. Arabella jumped up and flung the door wide.

"Larissa – how l-lovely! Do come in. It's a b-bit crowded, but there's plenty of t-tea in the p-pot."

Larissa was given a chair and offered tea and introduced to the room in general. "Just say 'Hi'," Arabella advised her. "You'll never remember all their names."

Larissa looked round her. "These are all your friends?" she wanted to know.

Arabella nodded. "Well, yes – you see, we all started our training together, and we stay in a bunch until we take our Finals – it's nice really because there's always someone to go out with or to share study." She sat down on the floor beside the Dutch girl. "Are you staying in London?"

"Just for a few days – I wish to buy clothes before our wedding and I do so like your Marks and Spencers, also I wish to see Billy and Sally – you have seen them?"

"Several times; they come here for treatment, you see, and I slip down and say hullo – they're doing awfully well. They'll be so glad to see you."

"Yes? I am glad. George misses you."

Arabella felt a wave of nostalgia sweep over for the old house in Doesburg. "And Tatters and Crosby and the kittens?" her voice was too bright. "And Emma, of course, and Hanneke. . . ."

"They all flourish. Arabella, I came to see if you would come and have dinner with me at my hotel." Larissa looked at her a little uncertainly and then at the over-full room.

"I'd love to." Perhaps Larissa would talk about Gideon. "I've had supper once," she went on with engaging frankness, "but it was beans on toast and I can easily forget it." She hesitated. "Are you alone – there isn't anyone. . .?"

"I am alone this evening – Gideon is over here too, but he has his own business to attend to – other fish to fry, do you not say? I am quite sure that we shall not see him this evening."

Arabella nodded; she had remembered that Hilary had told her, days ago, that she would be going out on this particular evening – it wasn't hard now to guess with whom it would be. She sprang to her feet, crying:

"I'm going out with Larissa, everyone. F-finish the tea if you w-want to."

She carved her way through her friends to the wardrobe and pulled out the tweed coat, caught up her gloves and handbag, and pausing only briefly before the mirror, declared herself to be ready. It was fortunate that she had worn the jersey dress that evening and had done her face and hair before she had gone down to supper. She waited at the door while Larissa, Dutch custom dying hard, shook hands with simply everyone in the room, and then accompanied her guest to the hospital entrance.

"There's a bus at the end of the road," volunteered Arabella. "Where do you want to go?"

But Larissa had already waved to a waiting taxi. "I told him to wait," she explained as they got in, and Arabella asked where they were going.

"Duke's Hotel, in St. James Place – it is quiet there."

Arabella had walked past it on a number of occasions – quiet indeed, and expensive too, she thought, but Larissa wouldn't have to worry about that. "How long are you here?" she asked.

"A few days only, then I fly to Lisbon to meet Dirk. Gideon will go home very shortly, I believe. Those were nice girls in your room – it is pleasant to have friends." She turned to smile at Arabella. "But have you not one particular friend?"

"Well, I suppose Anne is," replied Arabella promptly. "She's my closest friend – she has the room next to mine. She was the one with the dark hair sitting on my bed. We share things, you know, and help each other out and lend each other things."

Larissa laughed. "So she is as familiar with your possessions as you are."

"Oh, yes – she knows more or less where I keep everything, just as I know where all her things are. It's

180

handy, you know."

There was no need for Larissa to answer this, for the taxi had drawn up in front of the hotel and they got out and went inside. It was as nice as Arabella had imagined it would be; they went up to Larissa's room and tidied themselves without haste, then went in to dinner, during which meal Larissa showed herself to be an excellent conversationalist, touching on every topic under the sun, but never one word about her brother. They sat a long time over their meal until Arabella declared that she must return to the hospital. "Though it's lucky I'm not on duty until ten o'clock tomorrow," she explained.

"Until when will you work?" asked Larissa.

"Eight in the evening."

Larissa looked horrified. "But that is a very long day – you will be exhausted!"

"Perhaps. I don't do anything when I come off, only have supper and go to bed."

"Do you not find the days dull?"

"No, not really, not each day as it comes. Only sometimes when I think of year after year." She looked away, staring blindly at the opposite wall, seeing year after year slide by without seeing Gideon again.

"You are sad?" asked Larissa.

Arabella pinned a smile on her face. "Me? I'm thinking about tomorrow; theatre day and so busy. It's been lovely seeing you again. Will you write and tell me about your wedding?"

"Of course."

As she was getting into the taxi Arabella paused,

fought the returning stammer and said: "When you s-
see D-Doctor van der Vorst, p-please give him my r-
regards."

She was borne away and Larissa stood watching until
the taxi was out of sight and then went upstairs, only this
time she went to the room next to her own, where
Gideon was waiting.

It was almost eight o'clock in the evening of the following day. Arabella had coaxed, badgered and urged the
last of the up patients back into their beds, set the junior
nurses to a final tidying up, supplied Sister, still writing
in her office, with the last odds and ends of information
needed for the report, and gone back to old Mr. Reeves'
bed to check the ordered clutter of apparatus around
him. Everything was just as it should be. She stood looking at him tiredly, listening to the soft swish of the night
nurses' uniforms as they came down the corridor. She
might as well go. She heard the junior nurses wish Sister
good night, exchange greetings with the night nurses,
and go on their way – she might as well do the same. She
turned round, straight into Gideon, standing so close
that she bumped into his waistcoat, and shocked into
immobility, stood staring at it. But she raised her eyes to
his face when he said: "Hello, dear girl, how fortunate
that I should find you here." He beamed down at her,
very much at ease.

"Why?" she managed.

"I thought you might like a lift to see Nanny Bliss this
evening."

Her eyes went back to the waistcoat. Hilary hadn't been in the canteen; she hadn't seen her all day – she was home on days off and Gideon had come to see her and finding her gone, was going after her. He was, thought Arabella, a persistent man.

"Thank you, but I can't – I haven't a day off tomorrow."

"I have to be back myself this evening," he told her easily. "If we leave within half an hour that should give us ample time." He added with a calm placidity which she found very soothing after the hurry and bustle of the day, "Nanny will enjoy the surprise."

She was a fool to be persuaded, Arabella told herself; she had meant never to see him again, and here she was contemplating spending the evening with him – well, not quite that; he was offering her a lift to see Nanny because he was going to Little Dean House anyway to see Hilary – probably he would want to talk about her all the way there and all the way back.

"Thank you, I'll come," she said, her eyes on his tie so that she failed to see the gleam in his eyes. "Where do you want me to meet you?"

"At the entrance – don't worry about supper, we'll get something quick on the way." He glanced at his watch. "Can you get away now?"

"Yes, I'm off duty." She clapped a hand over her mouth like a little girl. "My goodness, does Sister know you're here?"

"Indeed she does. I've been here all the afternoon; I

made a point of asking her if I might see you in the ward."

"All the afternoon?" Why hadn't he driven hotfoot after Hilary?

As though he had read her thoughts, he said blandly: "I had a meeting to attend."

She nodded. "Well then – I'm ready."

"Bring a warm coat with you, it's cold outside."

It didn't take her half an hour to change into a sweater and skirt, the tweed coat again and her boots. She did her hair and face and then surveyed herself in the mirror; very neat but so deadly dull – not that it would matter in the least. She smiled a little though as she ran downstairs. It had mattered once; it seemed a long time ago now.

The Bentley stood, sleek and powerful, outside the hospital entrance, and inside it was deliciously warm and comfortable. She settled back against its soft leather with a little sigh as Gideon switched on the engine. "Why not close your eyes?" he suggested as they slipped into the stream of traffic. "And go to sleep properly this time," he added on a laugh.

"I'm not in the least sleepy." Arabella's voice was sharp because he had reminded her about an evening she wanted to forget – the evening when he had met Hilary. Perhaps he hadn't heard her; he began to talk, embarking on a gentle monologue about nothing which mattered. His deep, quiet voice lulled her over-active brain; she was asleep within five minutes.

She wakened as the doctor was driving the Bentley aboard the Harwich car ferry, and was, as might be expected, thunderstruck. But she was a sensible girl, and wasted no time in asking: "Where am I?" because she recognised her surroundings quite easily, nor did she say: "Why are we here?" because obviously Gideon knew what he was about; the most raw of motorists wouldn't have got lost to that extent, and he was no fool in a car. So she said with calm deliberation: "I don't know what you're doing, but I have no intention of going an inch further."

Which she realized at once was a silly remark, for the car was already nosing its elegant way forward into the queue of cars on the ferry car deck.

"I have no passport," she pointed out in the loud, clear voice one might use when addressing someone who had taken leave of his senses.

"It's in my pocket," said Gideon blandly, preparing to leave the car.

Arabella put out an urgent hand in its slightly shabby glove and caught at his coat sleeve. "But how.... Who gave it to you?"

"A friend of yours – Anne someone or other. I was to tell you that she will be able to wear the hat again, after all – whatever that means."

The stammer took over. "The t-traitor!" said Arabella fiercely. "T-take me b-back at once!"

For answer he opened the car door and got out, then walked round to help her out too. They were surrounded by cars now; he glanced around and shrugged enormous shoulders. "My dear little love," he said to take her breath, "how can I? Besides, I don't wish to do that. You see, I'm abducting you."

185

Arabella stared at him, bereft for the moment of speech, but he said nothing more, only took her arm and drew her towards the stairs leading to the deck above.

"W-what did you s-say?" Arabella managed at last.

"That I was abducting you, my little love." He stopped at the bottom of the stairs, oblivious of the people squeezing past them. "And now you are going to your cabin, where you will sleep until you are called in the morning."

She just managed not to wring her hands. "Gideon, oh, Gideon, you can't know what you're doing! What about Hilary – and poor Nanny? I can't go to sleep without knowing. . . ."

He caught her hands in his. "My dearest little darling, Hilary means nothing, she never has done, you know. If you had used your dear ears and eyes you would have known that, but you were so determined that I should fall in love with her, were you not, darling Arabella? And as for Nanny, she is waiting for us at Doesburg."

Arabella repeated his words soundlessly. At last she managed: "Gideon, why did you do it?"

He smiled with great tenderness. "Later, my darling. Do you know your Browning? You do? Then recollect the bit which goes 'Escape me? Never, Beloved, while I am I and you are you'. . . ."

"'So long as the world contains us both'," whispered Arabella. "Oh, Gideon!"

"Oh, Arabella!" He tucked her hand under an arm and walked her to the deck above where he handed her over to a fatherly steward who led her to a cabin and told her that he would be bringing her a little something on a tray as the gentleman had ordered, before she went to bed.

She ate her supper when it came because she was famished by now, while her thoughts chased themselves round and round inside her head, and she too tired to sort them out. She was in her bunk with her eyes resolutely closed when there was a tap on the door and Gideon came in.

"You've eaten your supper?" he enquired in a matter-of-fact voice. "Now, no more thinking, but go to sleep. We'll talk in the morning." He bent his head and kissed her very gently. "I'm next door if you want anything – just knock on the wall. Now close your eyes, my darling, and sleep. I fancy from the look of you that you haven't been sleeping very well lately."

Arabella had closed her eyes obediently. Without opening them now she said crossly: "Well, of course I haven't." Two tears oozed their way from under her lids and trickled down her cheeks and became, in no time at all, a flood. Gideon sat down on the bunk and gathered her close, saying nothing at all while she sobbed and sniffed in a tired way. Presently she grew calmer, and because she was so worn out with her feelings, she fell asleep, not stirring when he kissed her gently, laid her back on her pillow, and went quietly away.

They met for breakfast in the morning, and Gideon was still so matter-of-fact that she began to wonder if she had dreamed it all, but when the ship had docked and they were on their way down to the car deck, he said: "My darling, this is no place to talk. Will you wait a little longer, until we are home?"

She looked at him with puffy eyes; she was pale although she had slept. She felt very plain and slightly lightheaded. They were beside the Bentley now. As he opened the door for her he smiled down at her.

"You are the most beautiful girl in the world," he told her. "Get in, dear girl."

Arabella got in, aglow with the certainty that for him at least she was indeed beautiful. She sat beside him, content to let him talk trivialities while her thoughts wandered; quiet thoughts now, and happy ones. Even the quiet countryside looked beautiful as Gideon drove rapidly towards Doesburg.

The house was all that she had remembered; it was like coming home, and when Gideon opened the door and she went inside with his arm around her and she saw Emma standing there with Nanny beside her, Arabella almost choked with the strength of her feelings.

"Nanny!" she cried breathlessly. "Oh, Nanny, why are you here? I don't understand anything at all – I thought you were at Little Dean House – and are you well again?"

"Never better," declared Nanny, "and happy to be here. Me and Emma and that niece of hers, we get on very well, and when the babies come along, the doctor says I can have a good, hardworking girl to give me a hand."

"The babies?" uttered Arabella, completely bewildered.

Gideon's arm tightened around her. He said on a laugh: "Nanny Bliss has promised to come and live here with us, my darling, and of course it is unthinkable that she should have nothing to do; I thought that perhaps later – a handful of little Arabellas. . .?"

"But you haven't even asked me ... you can't say things like that." The look on his face stopped her; love, tenderness, gentle amusement – they were all there. She found herself saying: "And one or two handsome little Gideons. . . ."

He walked her to the sitting room, saying something to Emma as he went. He shut the door behind him, undid her coat and cast it from her and swept her close. "You will wish me to begin at the beginning," he said, "but I can't remember where the beginning was – not any more. I think I loved you when I looked into that bus and saw you standing there, grubby and frightened, but I didn't know it then. I knew it when I took you back to England and Hilary told me that you were going to marry Bertie – your girlhood sweetheart, she called him – and for quite a while I believed her. But that didn't mean that I was going to let you go." He paused to tighten his hold and kiss her thoroughly. "And you, my dear darling, matchmaking with all the fervour of a Victorian mama, under the mistaken impression that because ninety-nine men had fallen under Hilary's spell, the hundredth would too. So I played your game, my darling. That way I could see you, though I must say you led me a tiresome dance!"

Arabella lifted her head from the comfort of his shoulder. "You were b-beastly," she reminded him with slight pettishness. "You thought I wouldn't go and see

Nanny. . . ." She was unable to say any more because the doctor was kissing her again.

"My love," he said humbly, "you must forgive me for that; I lost my temper and my patience, and deep inside me I knew it wasn't true, and there you were, sitting up in bed looking so sweet."

Arabella smiled, finding the explanation most satisfactory. "Now tell me why you abducted me." She remembered something: "Larissa?"

"Such a help," murmured the doctor blandly. "So was your friend Anne – Sir Justin too."

"Sir Justin? But why? What did he do?"

"Made it easy for you to resign, my love, as from yesterday." He smiled a little. "You see, abducting you has saved such a lot of explanation."

Arabella stretched up to kiss him. "You don't mind that I stammer?" she asked a trifle anxiously.

"No, dear love – besides, you seldom do when you're with me. I find it one of your many charms – you are a girl of many charms."

"Am I really?" She was entranced at the very idea, and then struck by a sudden thought: "Gideon, what are we going to do?"

"Get married, my darling, as soon as I can arrange it. You will marry me, Arabella?"

It was surprising what love could do to a quite ordinary face. "Yes, dear Gideon – oh, I will, I will! It's like magic, isn't it?"

"Yes, my darling, it is magic." He kissed her once more very gently. "The magic of living."

The Essie Summers Story

One of the world's most popular and admired authors of romantic fiction, and a special favourite of all Harlequins readers, tells her story.

Essie Summers, the author of such best selling books as "Bride in Flight", "Postscript to Yesterday", "Meet on my Ground" and "The Master of Tawhai" to name just a few, has spent two years bringing the manuscript of her autobiography to its present stage of perfection.

The wit, warmth and wisdom of this fine lady shine, through every page. Her love of family and friends, of New Zealand and Britain, and of life itself is an inspiration throughout the book. Essie Summers captures the essence of a life well lived, and lived to the fullest, in the style of narrative for which she is justly famous.

"The Essie Summers Story", published in paperback, is available at .95 a copy through Harlequin Reader Service, now!